A Highland Parish

Morning in the Highlands.

Highlands.

FRONTISPIECE.

A

HIGHLAND PARISH.

By the
R**ev**. NORMAN MACLEOD, D.D.,
AUTHOR OF
" WEE DAVIE," " PARISH PAPERS," ETC.

NEW-YORK :
Robert Carter & Brothers,
530 Broadway.
1867.

THE sketches and stories that compose this volume are selected from Dr. MACLEOD'S "REMINISCENCES OF A HIGHLAND PARISH."

Those that feel an interest in a remarkable people who are rapidly passing away, will read these truthful sketches and simple tales with great delight, while such as have witnessed scenes akin to those described, will acknowledge that the pictures are drawn by a master hand.

Contents.

vi Contents.

A

HIGHLAND PARISH.

I.

The Highlands.

"There, westward away, where roads are unknown to
  Loch Navish,
And the great peaks look abroad over Skye to the
  westernmost islands."

THE Highlands of Scotland, like many
greater things in the world, may be
said to be unknown, yet well known. They
are known to the thousands of summer tourists who, every year, and from every part of
the civilized world, gaze on the romantic
beauties of the Trossachs and Loch Lomond,
skirt the Hebrides from the Firth of Clyde to
Oban, trundle through the wild gorge of

Glencoe, chatter among the ruins of Iona,
scramble over the wonders of Staffa, sail
along the magnificent line of lakes to Inver-
ness, reach the sombre Coolins, and disturb
the silence of Coruisk. Pedestrians, also,
with stick and knapsack, search the more solitary wilderness and glens of the mainland,
from the Grampians to Ross-shire and Caith-
ness. Sportsmen, too, whether real or only
make-believe, have their summer quarters in
the Highlands dotted over every moor, scattered on hill-sides and beside clear streams,
with all the irregularity of the boulders of
the great northern drift, but furnished with
most of the luxuries of an English home. All
these strangers, it must be admitted, know
something of the Highlands.

The tourists know the names of steamers,
coaches, and hotels; and how they were
cheated by boatmen, porters, or guides.
They have a vague impression of misty
mountains, stormy seas, heavy rain, difficult
roads, crowded inns, unpronounceable Gaelic
names, with brighter remembrances of land-

scapes whose grandeur they have probably never seen surpassed. Pedestrians can recall lonely and unfrequented paths across broken moorlands undulating far away, like broken shoreless seas, and through unploughed and untrodden valleys, where the bark of a shepherd's dog, and much more the sight of a shepherd's hut, were welcomed; and they cannot forget panoramas, from hill-tops, or from rocky promontories, of lake and river, moor and forest, sea and island, sunshine and cloud, of lonely keeps and ruined homesteads, of infinite sheep-walks and silent glens which seemed to end in chaos — remembrances which will come to them like holy days of youth, to refresh and sanctify, and "hang about the beatings of the heart" amidst the din and fret of a city life. Sportsmen, too, in a sense, know the Highlands. They have waded up to the shoulders in Highland lakes, nothing visible but hat swathed with flies, and hand wielding the little rod and line. They have trod the banks and tried the pools of every famous stream, until the very sal-

mon that are left know their features and
their flies, and tremble for.their cunning
temptations.   Or, quitting lake and stream,
they have sped with haste to stand upon the
Twelfth, at dawn of day, upon the blooming
heather. When they visit old shootings, they
hail from afar the well-known hill-sides, and
familiar "ground."   They can tell twenty
miles off where birds are scarce, or where, according to the state of the weather, they can
be found.   The whole scenery is associated in
their memory with the braces that have been
bagged, the stags which have been killed,
or—oh, horrid memory!—missed, "when
the herd was coming right towards us,
and all from that blockhead Charlie, who
would look if they were within shot." The
keepers, and gillies, and beaters, and the
whole tribe of expectants, are also well
known, *as such*, and every furrowed face is
to those sportsmen a very poem, an epic, a
heroic ballad, a history of the past season of
happiness and breezy hills, as well as a proph-
ecy of the morrow which is hoped for with

beating heart, that blames the night and urges on the morn.

There are others, too, who may be expected to know something of the Highlands. Low-country sheep-farmers, redolent of wool; English proprietors, who as summer visitants occupy the old house or castle of some extinct feudal chief; and antiquaries who have dipped into, or even studied profoundly, the civil and ecclesiastical antiquities of the land. Nevertheless, to each and all such the Highlands may be as unknown in their real life, as the scent of the wild bog myrtle is to the accomplished gentleman who has no sense of smell; or as a Gaélic boat-song in its words and spirit is to a Hindoo pundit.

Some of our readers may very naturally be disposed to ask, with a sneer of contempt, what precise loss any human being incurs from want of the knowledge? The opinion may be most reasonably held and expressed that the summer tourist, the wandering pedestrian, or the autumnal sportsman, have probably taken out of the Northern wilderness all that was worth bringing into the Southern Canaan of civilized life, and that as much gratitude, at least, is due for what is forgotten as for what is remembered.

Perhaps those readers may be right. And if so, then, for their own comfort as well as for ours, we ought to warn them that if they have been foolish enough to accompany us thus far, they should pity us, bid us farewell, and wish us a safe deliverance from the mountains.

Is there any one, let us ask, who reads those lines, and yet who dislikes peat-reek? any one who puts his fingers in his ears when he hears the bag-pipe—the real war-pipe—begin a real pibroch? any one who dislikes the kilt, the Gaelic, the clans, and who does not believe in Ossian? any one who has a prejudice to the Mac, or who cannot comprehend why one Mac should prefer a Mac of his own clan to the Mac of any other Clan? any one who smiles at the ignorance of a Highland parson who never reads the *Saturday Review* or the *Westminster*, who never heard about one in ten of the "schools of modern thought," and who believes, without any mental suffering, that two and two make four? any one who puts his glass to his eye during prayer in a Highland church, and looks at his fellow-traveler with a smile while the peasants sing their Psalms? any one who, when gazing on a Highland landscape, descants to his local admirers about some hackneyed Swiss scene *they* never saw, or enumerates a dozen Swiss *Horns*, the Wetter Horn, Schreckhorn, or any other horn which has penetrated into his brain? Forbid that any such terribly clever and well-informed cosmopolitans should "lose ten tickings of their watch" in reading these reminiscences!

One other class sometimes found in society, we would especially beseech to depart; we mean Highlanders ashamed of their country. Cockneys are bad enough, but they are sincere and honest in their idolatry of the Great Babylon. Young Oxonians or young barristers, even when they become slashing London critics, are more harmless than they themselves imagine, and after all inspire less awe than Ben Nevis, or than the celebrated agriculturist who proposed to decompose that mountain with acids, and to scatter the debris as a fertilizer over the Lochamber moss. But a Highlander born, who has been nurtured on oatmeal porridge and oatmeal cakes; who in his youth wore home-spun cloth, and was innocent of shoes and stockings; who blushed in his attempts to speak the English language; who never saw a nobler building for years than the little kirk in the glen, and who owes all that makes him tolerable in society to the Celtic blood which flows in spite of him through the veins;—for this man to be proud of his English accent, to sneer at the everlasting hills, the old kirk and its simple worship, and to despise the race which has never disgraced him—faugh! Peat-reek is frankincense in comparison with him; let him not be distracted by any of our reminiscences of the old country; leave us, we beseech of thee!

We ask not how old or how young those

are who remain with us; we care not what
their theory of political economy or their
school of modern philosophy may be; we are
indifferent as to their evening employment,
whether it be darning stockings, sitting idle
round the wintry fire in the enjoyment of repose, or occupying, as invalids, their bed·or
chair. If only they are charitable souls, who
hope all things and are not easily provoked;
who would like a peep into forms of society,
and to hear about people and customs differ-
ing in some degree from what they have
hitherto been acquainted with; to have an
easy chat about a country less known, perhaps, to them than any other in Europe,—
then shall we gladly unfold to them our reminiscences of a country and people worth
knowing about and loving, and of a period
in their history that is passing, if, indeed, it
has not already passed away.

And now, by way of further preamble to
our Reminiscences, let us take a bird's-eye
view of the parish. It is not included, by
Highland ecclesiastical statists, among what

are called the large parishes. We have no
idea of the number of square miles, of arable
acres, or of waste land, which it contains;
but science and the trigonometrical survey
will, it is presumed, give those details in due
time. When viewed as passing tourists view it,
from the sea, it has nothing remarkable about
it, and if it is pronounced by these same tourists to be uninteresting, and "just the sort of
scenery one would like to pass when dining
or sleeping," we won't censure the judgment.
A castled promontory, a range of dark precipices supporting the upland pastures, and
streaked with white waterfalls, that are lost
in the copse at their base, form a picture not
very imposing when compared with "what
one sees everywhere." A long ridge of hill
rising some two thousand feet above the sea,
its brown sides, up to a certain height, cheq-
uered with green stripes and patches of cul-
tivation; brown heather-thatched cottages,
with white walls; here and there a mansion,
whose chimneys are seen above the trees
which shelter it : these are its chief features

along the seaboard of twenty miles. But
how different is the whole scene when one
lands! New beauties reveal themselves, and
every object seems to change in size, appearance, and relative postion. A rocky wall of
wondrous beauty, the rampart of the old upraised beach which girdles Scotland, runs
along the shore ; the natural wild wood of ash,
oak, and birch, with the hazel copse, clothe
the lower hills and shelter the herds of wandering cattle; lonely sequestered bays are
everywhere scooped out into beautiful har-
bors; points and promontories seem to grow
out of the land, and huge dykes of whinstone
fashion to themselves the most picturesque
outlines ; clear streams everywhere hasten on
to the sea; small glens, perfect gems of
beauty, open up their entrances into the wonders of endless waterfalls and deep dark
pools, hemmed in by steep banks hanging
with ivy, honeysuckle, rowan-trees, and
ferns ; while on the hill-sides such signs of culture and industry as scattered cottages, small

farms, and shepherds' huts, give life to the whole scene.

Let us first look northward. Almost at our feet is a chain of small lakes, round whose green shores, unseen from the Cairn because immediately beneath it, a prosperous tenantry once lived, of whom no trace remains, except those patches of ruins which mark their once happy homesteads. Ruins there are, too, which show us that whatever defects the Church before the Reformation had accumulated, she excelled the Church of the present in the greater number and beauty of her parish churches. There are few sights which more rebuke the vulgar Church parsimony of these later days, or which imbue us with more grateful and generous feelings towards the missionaries of an earlier and more difficult time, than the faith and love which reared so many chapels on distant islands, and so many beautiful and costly fabrics in savage wildernesses, among a people who were too rude to appreciate such works, or the spirit which originated them. These old

Highland Church extensionists were not stim-
ulated by party rivalry, public meetings, or
newspaper articles. Their praise could not
have been from men. How they got the
means and money we know not, but this we
believe, that

> "They dreamt not of a perishable home
>   Who thus could build !"

But to view the parish in all its outward
aspect, we must ascend to the top of ———

> "I name not its name, lest inquisitive tourists
> Hunt it, and make it a lion, and get it at last into
>   guide-books."

The upward path soon leaves the cultivated
settlements, passes several streams, winds
across tracts of moorland, and at last reaches
the shieldings of Corrie Borrodale. One cannot imagine a sweeter spot than this in which
to repose before attempting the proper ascent
of the hill. A stream, clear as a diamond,
and singing its hill song, takes a sweep, and

folds within its embrace a bay of emerald
grass, surrounded with blooming heather.
Here and there appear small groups of ruins,
mere gatherings of stones, to mark where
man once built his temporary home. Before
sheep-farming was introduced generally into
the Highlands, about sixty or seventy years
ago, the cattle ranged through the hills as
high up as the grass grew, and it was necessary, during summer to follow them thither,
to milk them there, and make up stores of
butter and cheese for winter use. This led to
the building of those summer *chálets*, which
were managed chiefly by women and herd-
boys, but visited often, perhaps daily, by the
mistress of the farm, who took the dairy under her special charge. Thus it is that when
one rests in such a green oasis, his fancy again
peoples the waste with the herd-lads " calling
the cattle home," and with the blythe girls
who milked the cattle; he sees again the life
among the huts, and hears the milk-songs
and innocent glee; and when awakened from
his reverie by bleating sheep—the only living

tenants of the pastures, he is not disposed to
admit the present time to be an improvement
on the past.

But let us up to that green spot beside the
ravine ; then to the left along the rocks, then
to the right till past the deep " peat-bogs,"
and finally straight up to the Cairn. When
we have taken breath, let us look around.
This is the very high altar of the parish, and
we maintain that all the glories which can be
seen from a parish, rightfully belong to the
parish itself, and are a part of its own rich in-
heritance.

But to our picture again. Opposite to the
spectator, and rising abruptly from the valley,
is a range of hills, broken into wild scaurs
and clothed with copse ; while beyond these,
rise, ridge on ridge, like a mighty ocean sea,
heaving in gigantic billows onwards Ben
Reshapol, until lost to sight beyond the head
of Loch Shiel and among the braes of Lochaber. Sweeping the eye from the north, to the
west, what a glorious spectacle ! The chain
of lakes beneath end in the lovely Loch

Sunart, with its beauteous bays and wooded
islets. Over its farther shore, belonging to
that huge parish and huge word Ardnamurchan, and above picturesque hills, the more
distant Hebrides rear their heads out of the
ocean. Along the horizon southwards are
seen, the Scur of Eigg lifting its gigantic pil-
lar, the dark lines of Rum, and the islands of
Canna, Coll, and Tiree, the gleams of the
ocean between. The long dark moorland ascent by which we have reached the hill-top,
now carries the eye down to the sea. That
is a strait, worming itself for more than
twenty miles between the mainland where we
stand, and the island of Mull, which gathers
up its hills into a cluster of noble peaks about
its centre, with Bentealbh (Bentalve) and
Benmore towering over all. A low isthmus
right opposite, opens up an arm of the sea beyond Mull, with noble headlands, beneath
which the man who would see Staffa aright
should sail out to the ocean with no strangers
save a Highland crew; for not from crowded
steamer can he fully understand that pillared

island and its cathedral cave. Let us take one other glance to the east—the eye following the Sound of Mull, and our panorama is completed. How nobly the Sound, dotted with vessels, opens up past Ardtornish and Duart Castles, ere it mingles with the broader waters that sweep in eddying tides past the Slate Isles, past Jura, Scarba, on to Islay, until they finally spread out into the roll and roar of the shoreless Atlantic. In that western distance may be seen some white smoke that marks Oban, and over it Ben Cruachan, the most beautiful of our western hills, accompained by its grey companions, " the shepherds of Etive Glen."

We back this view from the highest hill in the parish for extent and varied beauty against any view in Europe ! It is the Righi of Argyleshire; and given only, what, alas ! is not easily obtained, a good day, good in transparency, good with " gorgeous cloudland," good with lights and shadows, the bright blue of the northern sky (more intense than the Italian), looking down and mingling with

the sombre dark of the northern hills, dark
even when relieved in autumn by the glow of
the purple heather—given all this, and we
know not where to find a more magnificent
outlook over God's fair earth. No reminiscences of the outer world so haunt our memory as those so often treasured up from that
grey cairn ; and however frequently we have
returned from beholding other and more famous scenes, this one has appeared like a first
love, only more beautiful than them all.

As we descend from the hill, the minister—
how oft has he gone with us there !—tells us
stories worth hearing, and as he alone can tell
them ; stories of a pastor's life, "from perils
in the wilderness, and perils of waters, and
perils of the sea ;" stories of character, such
as the lonely hills and misty moors alone can
mould ; stories of combats among the wild
and primitive inhabitants of the olden time ;
and stories, too, of the early invaders of the
land from Denmark and Norway, sea-kings,
or pirates rather, whose names yet linger

where they fell in battle, as at Corrie *Borrodale*, Corrie *Lundie*, and Ess *Stangadal*.

But we have reached "the manse;" and from thence we must start with our reminiscences of "A Highland Parish."

II.

The Manse.

"Say, ye far-travelled clouds, far-seeing hills—
  Among the happiest-looking homes of men
  Scatter'd all Britain over, through deep glen
On airy uplands, and by forest-rills,
And o'er wide plains, whereon the sky distils
  Her lark's loved warblings—does aught meet your ken
  More fit to animate the Poet's pen,
Aught that more surely by its aspect fills
Pure minds with sinful envy, than the abode
  Of the good Priest: who, faithful through all hours
To his high charge, and truly serving God,
  Has yet a heart and hand for trees and flowers,
Enjoys the walks his predecessors trod,
  Nor covets lineal rights in lands and towers?"

WORDSWORTH.

THERE lived in the Island of Skye, more than a century ago, a small farmer or "gentleman tacksman." Some of his admirably-written letters are now before me; but

I know little of his history beyond the fact revealed in his correspondence, and preserved in the affectionate traditions of his descendants, that he was "a good man," and the first within the district where he lived who introduced the worship of God in his family.

One great object of his ambition was to give his sons the best education that could be obtained for them, and in particular to train his first-born for the ministry of the Established Church of Scotland. His wishes were fully realized, for the noble institution of the parochial school provided in the remotest districts of Scotland teaching of a very high order, and produced admirable classical scholars—such as even Dr. Johnson talks of with respect.

Besides the schools, there was an excellent custom then existing among the tenantry in Skye, of associating themselves to obtain a good tutor for their sons. The tutor resided alternately at different farms, and the boys from the other farms in the neighborhood came daily to him. In this way the burden of sup-

porting the teacher, and the difficulties of
travelling on the part of the boys, were divided among the several. families in the district. In autumn the tutor, accompanied
by his more advanced pupils, journeyed on
foot to Aberdeen to attend the University.
He superintended their studies during the
winter, and returned in spring with them to
their Highland homes to pursue the same
routine. The then Laird of Macleod was one
who took a pride in being surrounded by a
tenantry who possessed so much culture. It
was his custom to introduce all the sons of
his tenants who were studying in Aberdeen
to their respective professors, and to entertain
both professors and students in his house.
On one such occasion, when a professor remarked with surprise, " Why, sir, these are
all gentlemen !" Macleod replied, " Gentlemen I found them, as gentlemen I wish to see
them educated, and as gentlemen I hope to
leave them behind me."

The "gentleman tacksman's" eldest son
acted as a tutor for some time, and then be-

came minister of "the Highland Parish."
It was said of him that "a finer-looking or
prettier man never left his native island."
He was upwards of six feet in height, with a
noble countenance which age only made nobler. He was accompanied from Skye by a
servant-lad, whom he had known from his
boyhood, called "Rauri Beg," or little Rory.
Rory was rather a contrast to his master in
outward appearance. One eye was blind, but
the other seemed to have robbed the sight
from its extinguished neighbor to intensify its
own. That grey eye gleamed and scintillated
with the peculiar sagacity and reflection
which one sees in the eye of a Skye terrier,
but with such intervals of feeling as human
love of the most genuine kind could alone
have expressed. One leg, too, was slightly
shorter than the other, and the manner in
which Rory rose on the longer or sunk on the
shorter, and the frequency or rapidity with
which those alternate ups and downs in his
life were practised, became a telegraph of
Rory's thoughts when no words, out of respect

to his master, were spoken. "So you don't
agree with me, Rory?" "What's wrong?"
"You think it dangerous to put to sea to-
day?" "Yes; the mountain-pass also would
be dangerous? Exactly so. Then we must
consider what is to be done." These were
the sort of remarks which a series of slow or
rapid movements of Rory's limbs often drew
forth from his master, though no other token
was afforded of his inner doubt or opposition.
A better boatman, a truer genius at the helm,
never took a tiller in his hand; a more endur-
ing traveller never "gaed ower the moor
amang the heather;" a better singer of a boat-
song never cheered the rowers, nor kept them
as one man to their stroke; a more devoted,
loyal, and affectionate "minister's man" and
friend never lived than Rory—first called
"Little Rory," but as long as I can remenber.
"Old Rory." But more of him anon. The
minister and his servant arrived in the High·
land Parish nearly ninety years ago, almost
total strangers to its inhabitants, and alone

they entered the manse to see what it was like.

I ought to inform my readers that the Presbyterian Church is established in Scotland, and that the landed proprietors in each parish are bound by law to build and keep in repair a church, suitable school, and parsonage or "manse," and also to secure a portion of land, or "glebe," for the minister. Both the manses and churches have of late years immensely improved in Scotland, so that in many cases they are now far superior to those in some of the rural parishes of England. Much still remains to be accomplished in this department of architecture and taste! Yet even at the time I speak of, the manse was in its structure rather above than below the houses occupied by the ordinary gentry, with the exception of " the big house" of the Laird. It has been succeeded by one more worthy of the times; but the old manse was nevertheless respectable.

The glebe was the glory of the manse! It

was the largest in the county, consisting of about sixty acres, and containing a wonderful combination of Highland beauty. It was bounded on one side by a "burn," whose torrent rushed far down between lofty steep banks clothed with natural wood, ash, birch, hazel, oak, and rowan-tree, and poured its dark moss-water over a series of falls, and through deep pools, "with beaded bubbles winking at the brim." It was never tracked along its margin by any human being, except herd-boys and their companions, who swam the pools, and clambered up the banks, holding by the roots of trees, starting the king-fisher from his rock, or the wild cat from his den. On the other side of the glebe was the sea, with here a sandy beach, and there steep rocks and deep water; small grey islets beyond; with many birds, curlews, cranes, divers, and gulls of all sorts, giving life to the rocks and shore. Along the margin of the sea there stretched such a flat of green grass as suggested the name which it bore, of "the Duke of Argyle's walk." And pac-

ing along that green margin at evening,
what sounds and wild cries were heard of
piping sea-birds, chafing waves, the roll of
oars, and the song from fishing-boats, which
told of their return home. The green ter-
race - walk which fringed the sea, was but
the outer border of a flat that was hemmed
in by the low precipice of the old upraised
beach of Scotland. Higher still was a second
storey of green fields and emerald pastures,
broken by a lovely rocky knoll, called Fingal's hill, whose grey head, rising out of
green grass, bent towards the burn, and
looked down into his own image reflected in
the deep pools which slept as its feet. On
that upper table-land, and beside a clear
stream, stood the manse and garden sheltered
by trees. Beyond the glebe began the dark
moor, which swept higher and higher, until
crowned by the mountain-top of which I have
already spoken, which looked away to the
Western Islands and to the peaks of Skye.

The minister, like most of his brethren,
soon took to himself a wife, the daughter of

2

a neighboring "gentleman tacksman," and
the grand-daughter of a minister, well born,
and well bred ; and never did man find a help
more meet for him In that manse they both
lived for nearly fifty years, and his wife bore
him sixteen children ; yet neither father nor
mother could ever lay their hand on a child
of theirs and say, " We wish this one had not
been." They were all a source of unmingled
joy to them.

A small farm was added to the glebe, for it
was found that the machinery required to
work sixty acres of arable and pasture land
could work more with the same expense.
Besides, John Duke of Argyle made it a rule
at that time to give farms at less than their
value to the ministers on his estate ; and why,
therefore, should not our minister, with his
sensible, active, thrifty wife, and growing sons
and daughters, have a small one, and thus secure for his large household abundance of
food, including milk and butter, cheese, potatoes, meal, with the excellent addition of
mutton, and sometimes beef too ? And the

good man did not attend to his parish worse
when his living was thus bettered ; nor was
he less cheerful or earnest in duty when in
his house " there was bread enough and to
spare."

. The manse and glebe of that Highland parish were a colony which ever preached sermons, on week days as well as on Sundays, of
industry and frugality, of a courteous hospitality and a bountiful charity, and the domestic peace, contentment, and cheerfulness
of a holy Christian home. Several cottages
were built by the minister and clustered in
sheltered nooks near his dwelling. One or
two were inhabited by laborers and shepherds; another by the weaver, who made all
the carpets, blankets, plaids, and finer webs
of linen and woollen cloths required for the
household ; and another by old Jenny, the
hen-wife, herself like an old hen, waddling
about and *chucking* among her numerous
family of poultry. Old Rory, with his wife
and family, was located near the shore, to attend at spare hours to fishing, as well as to

be ready with the boat for the use of the minister in his pastoral work. Two or three cottages besides these were inhabited by objects of charity, whose claims upon the family it was difficult to ·trace. An old sailor had settled down in one, but no person could tell anything about him, except that he been born in Skye, had served in the navy, had fought at the Nile, had no end of stories for winter evenings, and spinned yarns about the wars and "foreign parts." He had come long ago in distress to the manse, from whence he had passed after a time into the cottage, and there lived a dependant on the family until he died twenty years afterwards. A poor decayed gentlewoman, connected with one of the old families of the county, and a tenth cousin of the minister's wife, had also cast herself in her utter loneliness, like a broken wave, on the glebe. She had only intended to remain a few days—she did not like to be troublesome—but she knew how she could rely on a blood relation, and she found it hard to leave,_ for whither could she go? And

those who had taken her in never thought of
bidding this sister " depart in peace, saying
Be ye clothed ;" and so she became a neighbor to the sailor, and was always called
" Mrs." Stewart, and was treated with the
utmost delicacy and respect, being fed, clothed
and warmed in her cottage with the best
which the manse could afford ; and when she
died, she was dressed in a shroud fit for a
lady, and tall candles, made for the occasion
according to the old custom, were kept lighted
round her body. Her funeral was becoming
the gentle blood that flowed in her veins ;
and no one was glad in their heart when she
departed, but they sincerely wept, and
thanked God she had lived in plenty and
had died in peace.

Within the manse the large family of sons
and daughters managed, somehow or other,
to accommodate not only themselves, but to
find permanent room also for a tutor and governess ; and such a thing as turning any one
away from want of room was never dreamt
of. When hospitality demanded such a

small sacrifice, the boys would all go to the barn, and the girls to the chairs and sofas of parlor and dining-room, with fun and laughter, joke and song, rather than not make the friend or stranger welcome. And seldom was the house without either. The "kitchen end," or lower house, with all its indoor crannies of closets and lofts, and outdoor additions of cottages, barns, and stables, was a little world of its own, to which wandering pipers, parish fools, the parish post, beggars, with all sorts of odd-and-end characters came, and where they ate, drank, and rested. As a matter of course, the "upper house" had its own set of guests to attend to. The traveller by sea, whom adverse winds and tides drove into the harbor for refuge ; or the traveller by land ; or any minister passing that way ; or friends on a visit ; or, lastly and but rarely, some foreign "Sassanach" from the Lowlands of Scotland or England, who dared then to explore the unknown and remote Highlands as one now does Montenegro or the Ural Mountains—all these found a hearty reception.

One of the most welcome visitors was the packman. His arrival was eagerly longed for by all, except the minister, who trembled for his small purse in presence of the prolific pack. For this same pack often required a horse for its conveyance. It contained a choice selection of everything which a family was likely to require from the lowland shops. The haberdasher and linendraper, the watchmaker and jeweller, the cutler and hairdresser, with sundry other crafts in the useful and fancy line, were all fully represented in the endless repositories of the pack. What a solemn affair was the opening up of that peripatetic warehouse! It took a few days to gratify the inhabitants of manse and glebe, and to enable them to decide how their money should be invested. The boys held sundry councils about knives, and the men about razors, silk handkerchiefs, or, it may be, about the final choice of a silver watch. The servants were in nervous agitation about some bit of dress. Ribbons, like rainbows, were unrolled; prints held up in graceful folds before the light; cheap shawls were displayed on the back of some handsome lass, who served as a model. There never was seen such new fashions or such cheap bargains! And then how "dear papa" was coaxed by mamma; and mamma again by her daughters. Everything was so beautiful, so tempting, and was discovered to be so necessary! All this time the packman, who was often of the stamp of him whom Wordsworth has made illustrious, was treated as a friend; while the news, gathered on his travels, was as welcome to the minister as his goods were to his family. No one in the upper house was so vulgar as to screw him down, but felt it due to his respectability to give him his own price, which, in justice to those worthy old merchants, I should state was always reasonable.

The manse was the grand centre to which all the inhabitants of the parish gravitated for help and comfort. Medicines for the sick were weighed out from the chest yearly replenished in Glasgow. They were not given in homœopathic doses, for Highlanders, accustomed to things on a large scale, would have had no faith in globules, and faith was half their cure. Common sense and common medicines were found helpful to health. The poor, as a matter of course, visited the manse, not for an order on public charity, but for aid from private charity, and it was never refused in *kind*, such as meal, wool, or potatoes. As there were no lawyers in the parish, lawsuits were adjusted in the manse; and so were marriages not a few. The distressed came there for comfort, and the perplexed for advice; and there was always something material as well as spiritual to share with them all. No one went away empty in body or soul. Yet the barrel of meal was never empty, nor the cruise of oil extinguished. A "wise" neighbor once remarked, "that minister with his large family will ruin himself, and if he dies they will be beggars." Yet there has never been a beggar among them to the fourth generation. No "saying" was more common in the mouth of this servant than the saying of his Master, "It is more blessed to give than to receive."

One characteristic of that manse life was its constant cheerfulness. One cottager could play the bagpipe, another the violin. The minister was an excellent performer on the violin. If strangers were present, so much the better. He had not an atom of that proud fanaticism which connects virtue with suffering, as suffering, apart from its cause.*

Here is an extract from a letter written

---

* A minister in a remote island parish once informed me that, " on religious grounds," he had broken the only fiddle in the island ! His notion of religion, we fear, is not rare among his brethren in the far west and north. We are informed by Mr. Campbell, in his admirable volumes on the Tales of the Highlands, that the old songs and tales are also being put under the clerical ban in some districts, as being too secular and profane for their pious inhabitants. What next ? Are the singing-birds to be shot by the kirk-sessions ?

by the minister in his old age, some fifty
years ago, which gives a very beautiful picture of the secluded manse and its ongoings.
It is written at the beginning of a new year,
in reply to one which he had received from
his first-born son, then a minister of the
Church :—

"What you say about the beginning of
another year is quite true. But, after all,
may not the same observations apply equally
well to every new day ? Ought not daily mercies to be acknowledged, and God's favor and
protection asked for every new day ? and are
we not as ignorant of what a new day as of
what a new year may bring forth ? There is
nothing in nature to make this day in itself
more worthy of attention than any other.
The sun rises and sets on it as on other days,
and the sea ebbs and flows. Some come into
the world and some leave it, as they did yesterday and will do to-morrow. On what day
may not one say, I am a year older than I was
this day last year ? Still I must own that
the first of the year speaks to me in a more

commanding and serious language than any other common day; and the great clock or time, which announced the first hour of this year, did not strike unnoticed by us.

"The sound was too loud to be unheard, and too solemn to pass away unheeded. We in the manse did not mark the day by any unreasonable merriment. We were alone, and did eat and drink with our usual innocent and cheerful moderation. I began the year by gathering all in the house and on the glebe to prayer. Our souls were stirred up to bless and to praise the Lord: for what more reasonable, what more delightful duty than to show forth our gratitude and thankfulness to that great and bountiful God from whom we have our years, and days, and all our comforts and enjoyments. Our lives have been spared till now; our state and conditions in life have been blessed; our temporal concerns have been favored; the blessing of God co-operated with our honest industry; our spiritual advantages have been great and numberless; we have had the means of grace and the hope of glory; in a word, we have had all that was requisite for the good of our body and soul; and shall not our souls and all that is within us, all our powers and faculties, be stirred up to bless and praise His name!

"But to return. This pleasant duty being gone through, refreshments were brought in, and had any of your clergy seen the crowd (say thirty, great and small, besides the family of the manse) they would pity the man who, under God, had to support them all! This little congregation being dismissed, they went to enjoy themselves. They entertained each other by turns. In the evening, I gave them one end of the house. We enjoyed ourselves in a different manner in the other end. Had you popped in unnoticed, you would see us all grave, quiet, and studious. You would see your father reading The Seasons; your mother, Porteous' Lectures; your sister Anne, The Lady of the Lake; and Archy, Tom Thumb!

"Your wee son was a new and great treat

to you in those bonny days of rational mirth and joy, but not a whit more so than you were to me at his time of life, nor can he be more so during the years to come. May the young gentleman long live to bless and comfort you! May he be to you what you have been and are to me! I am the last that can honestly recommend to you not to allow him get too strong a hold of your heart, or rather not to allow yourself to *dote too much* upon him. This was a peculiar weakness of my own, and of which I had cause more than once to repent with much grief and sore affliction. But your mother's creed always was (*and truly she has acted up to it*) to enjoy and delight in the blessings of the Almighty while they were spared to her, with a thankful and grateful heart, and to part with them when it was the will of the gracious Giver to remove them, with humble submission and meek resignation."

We will have something more to say in a coming chapter about this pastor and his work in the parish.

III.

The Boys of the Manse.

" Life went a-maying
With Nature, Hope, and Poesy
When I was young !
When I was young ?—Ah ! woful when ? "

COLERIDGE.

THE old minister had no money to leave his
boys when he died, and so he wisely. determined to give them while he lived, the
treasure of the best education in his power.
The first thing necessary for the accomplish-
ment of his object, was to obtain a good tutor,
and a good tutor was not difficult to get.

James, as we shall call the tutor of the
manse boys, was a laborious student, with a
most creditable amount of knowledge of the
elements of Greek and Latin.   When at college he was obliged to live in the top storey

of a high house in a murky street, breathing
an atmosphere of smoke, fog, and gas;
cribbed in a hot, close room; feeding on ill-
cooked meat (fortunately in small quantities);
drinking " coffee" half water, half chicory;
sitting up long after midnight writing essays
or manufacturing exercises, until at last dys-
pepsia depressed his spirits and blanched his
visage, except where it was colored by a hec-
tic flush, which deepened after a fit of cough-
ing.   When he returned home after having
carried off prizes in the Greek or Latin
classes, what cared ·his mother for all these
honors?   No doubt she was " prood oor
James," but yet she could hardly know her
boy, he had become so pale, so haggard, and
so unlike " himsel'."   What a blessing for
James to get off to the Highlands!   He there
breathed such air, and drank such water as
made him wonder at the bounty of creation
without taxation.   He climbed the hills and
dived into the glens, and rolled himself on the
heather; visited old castles, learned to fish,
and perhaps to shoot, shutting both eyes at ·

The Manse Boys Fishing.

Highlands.

p. 48.

first when he pulled the trigger. He began
to write verses, and to fall in love with one
or all of the young ladies. That was the sort
of life which Tom Campbell the poet passed
when sojourning in the West Highlands; ay,
for a time in this very parish too, where the
lovely spot is yet pointed out as the scene of
his solitary musings. James had a great de
light not only in imparting the rudiments of
language, but also in opening up various high
roads and outlying fields of knowledge. The
intellectual exercise braced himself, and delighted his pupils.

If ever " muscular Christianity" was taught
to the rising generation, the Highland manse
of these days was its gymnasium. After
school hours, and on " play-days" and Saturdays, there was no want of employment calculated to develop physical energy. The
glebe and farm made a constant demand for
labor, which it was joy to the boys to afford.
Every season brought its own appropriate
and interesting work. But sheep-clipping,
the reaping and ingathering of the crops, with

now and then the extra glory of a country
market for the purchase and sale of cattle;
with tents, games, gingerbread, horse jockeys,
and English cattle dealers,—these were their
great annual feasts.

The grander branches of education were
fishing, sailing, shooting,—game-laws being
then unknown—and also what was called
"hunting." The fishing I speak of was not
with line and fly on river or lake, though
that was in abundance; but it was sea-fishing
with rod and white fly for "Saith" and mackerel in their season. It was delightful towards
evening to pull for miles to the fishing-ground
in company with other boats. A race was
sure to be kept up both going and returning,
while songs arose from all hands and from
every boat, intensifying the energy of the
rowers. Then there was the excitement of
getting among a great play of fish, which
made the water foam for half a mile round,
and attracted flocks of screaming birds who
seemed mad with gluttony, while six or seven
rods had all at the same time their lines

tight, and their ends bent to cracking with
the sport; keeping every fisher hard at work
pulling in the fine lithe creatures, until the
bottom of the boat was filled with scores.
Sometimes the sport was so good as to in-
duce a number of boats' crews to remain all
night on a distant island, which had only a
few sheep, and a tiny spring of water. The
boats were made fast on the lee side, and
their crews landed to wait for daybreak.
Then began the fun and frolic!—"sky-lark-
ing," as the sailors called it, among the
rocks—pelting one another with clods and
wrack, or any harmless substance which
could be collected for the battle, amidst
shouts of laughter, until they were wearied,
and lay down to sleep in a sheltered nook,
and all was silent but the beating wave, the
"eerie" cries of birds, and the splash of some
sea-monster in pursuit of its prey. What
glorious reminiscences have I, too, of those
scenes, and specially of early morn, as
watched from those green islands! It seems
to me as if I had never beheld a true sunrise

since; yet how many have I witnessed! I left the sleeping crews, and ascended the top of the rock, immediately before daybreak, and what a sight it was, to behold the golden crowns which the sun placed on the brows of the mountain-monarchs who first did him homage; what heavenly dawnings of light on peak and scaur, contrasted with the darkness of the lower valleys; what gleams of glory in the eastern sky, changing the cold, grey clouds of early morning into bars of gold and radiant gems of beauty; and what a flood of light suddenly burst upon the dancing waves, as the sun rose above the horizon, and revealed the silent sails of passing ships; and what delight to see and hear the first break of the fish on the waters! With what pleasure I descended, and gave the cheer which made every sleeper awake, and scramble to their boats, and in a few minutes resume the work of hauling in our dozens! Then home with a will for breakfast—each striving to be first on the sandy shore!

Fishing at night with the drag-net was a sport which cannot be omitted in recording the enjoyments of the manse-boys. The spot selected was a rocky bay, or embouchure of a small stream. The night was generally dark and calm. The pleasure of the occupation was made up of the pull, often a long one, within the shadow of the rocky shore, with the calm sea reflecting the stars in the sky, and then the slow approach, with gently-moving oars, towards the beach, in order not to disturb the fish; the wading up to the middle to draw in the net when it had encircled its prey; and the excitement as it was brought into shallow water, the fish shining with their phosphoric light; until, at last, a grand haul of salmon-trout, flounders, small cod, and lithe, lay walloping in the folds of the net upon the sandy beach.

Those fishing excursions, full of incident as they were, did not fully test or develop the powers of the boys. But others were afforded capable of doing so. It was their delight to accompany their father on any

boat-journey which the discharge of his pastoral duties required. In favorable weather,
they had often to manage the boat themselves without any assistance. When the sky
was gloomy, old Rory took the command.
Such of my readers as have had the happiness—or the horror, as their respective tastes
may determine—to have sailed among the
Hebrides in an open boat, will be disposed
to admit that it is a rare school for disciplin-
ing its pupils when patient and conscientious
to habits of endurance, foresight, courage,
decision, and calm self-possession. The minister's boat was about eighteen feet keel,
undecked, and rigged fore and aft. There
were few days in which the little "Roe"
would not venture out, with Rory at the
helm; and with no other person would his
master divide the honor of being the most
famous steersman in those waters. But to
navigate her across the wild seas of that
stormy coast demanded "a fine hand"
which could only be acquired after years
of constant practice, such as a rider for the

Derby prides in, or a whipper-in during a
long run across a stiff country. If Rory
would have made a poor jockey, what jockey
would have steered the " Roe" in a gale of
wind? I can assure the reader it was a
solemn business, and solemnly was it gone
about! What care in seeing the ropes in
order; the sails reefed; the boys in their
right place at the fore and stern sheets; and
everything made snug. And what a sight
it was to see that old man when the
storm was fiercest, with his one eye, under
its shaggy grey brow, looking to windward,
sharp, calm, and luminous as a spark; his
hand clutching the tiller—never speaking a
word, and displeased if any other broke the
silence, except the minister who sat beside
him, assigning this post of honor as a great
favor to Rory, during the trying hour. That
hour was generally when wind and tide met,
and "gurly grew the sea," whose green
waves rose with crested heads, hanging
against the cloud-rack, and sometimes concealing the land; while black sudden

rushing down from the glens, struck the
foaming billows in fury, and smote the boat,
threatening, with a sharp scream, to tear the
tiny sails in tatters, break the mast, or blow
out of the water the small dark speck that
carried the manse treasures. There was one
moment of peculiar difficulty and concentrated danger when the hand of a master
was needed to save them. The boat has entered the worst part of the tideway. How
ugly it looks! Three seas higher than the
rest are coming; and you can see the squall
blowing their white crests into smoke. In
a few minutes they will be down on the
"Roe." "Look out, Rauri!" whispers the
minister. "Stand by the sheets!" cries Rory
to the boys, who, seated on the ballast, gaze
on him like statues, watching his face, and
eagerly listening in silence. "Ready!" is
their only reply. Down come the seas, rolling, rising, breaking; falling, rising again,
and looking higher and fiercer than ever.
The tide is running like a race-horse, and the
gale meets it; and these three seas appear

now to rise like huge pyramids of green
water, dashing their foam up into the sky.
The first may be encountered and overcome,
for the boat has good way upon her; but the
others will rapidly follow up the thundering
charge and shock, and a single false movement of the helm by a hair's-breadth will
bring down a cataract like Niagara that
would shake a frigate, and sink the "Roe"
into the depths like a stone. The boat meets
the first wave, and rises dry over it. "Slack
out the main sheet, quick, and hold hard;
there—steady!" commands Rory, in a low,
firm voice, and the huge back of the second
wave is seen breaking to leeward. "Haul
in, boys, and belay!" Quick as lightning
the little craft, having again gathered wind,
is up in the teeth of the wind, and soon is
spinning over the third topper, not a drop of
water having come over the lee gunwale.
"Nobly done, Rory!" exclaims the minister,
as he looks back to the fierce tideway which
they have passed. Rory smiles with satisfaction at his own skill, and quietly remarks of

the big waves, " They have *their* road, and I
have mine ! "   " Hurrah for the old boat ! "
exclaims one of the boys.   Rory repeats his
favorite aphorism—yet never taking his eye
off the sea and sky.—" Depend on it, my lads,
it is not boats that drown the men, but men
the boats !"   I take it that the old " Roe "
was no bad school for boys who had to battle
with the storms and tides of life.   I have
heard one of those boys tell, when old and
greyheaded, and after having encountered
many a life storm, how much he had owed to
those habits of mind which had been strengthened by his sea life with old Rory.

The " hunting " I have alluded to as affording another branch of out-door schooling, was
very different from what goes under that
sporting term in the south.   It was confined
chiefly to wild cats and otters.   The animals
employed in this work were terriers.   The
two terriers of the manse were " Gasgach "
or " Hero," and " Cuilag " or " Fly."   They
differed very considerably in character : Gasgach was a large terrier with wiry black and

grey hairs; Cuilag was of a dusky brown,
and so small that she could be carried in the
pocket of a shooting jacket. Gasgach presumed not to enter the parlor, or to mingle
with genteel society; Cuilag always did so,
and lay upon the hearth-rug, where she
basked and reposed in state. Gasgach was a
sagacious, prudent, honest police sergeant,
who watched the house day and night, and
kept the farm-dogs in awe, and at their respective posts. He was also a wonderful de-
tective of all beggars, rats, fumarts, wild
cats, and vermin of every kind, smelling afar
off the battle with man or beast. Cuilag was
full of *reticence*, and seemed to think of nothing, or do nothing until *seriously* wanted;
and then indomitable courage started from
every hair in her body. Both had seen constant service since their puppyhood, and
were covered with honorable scars from the
nose to the tip of the tail; each cut being the
record of a battle, and the subject of a story
by the boys.

The otters in the parish were both numerous, large, and fierce.   There was one famous den called "Clachoran," or the otter's stone, composed of huge rocks, from which the sea wholly receded during spring-tides. Then was the time to search for its inhabitants.   This was done by the terriers driving the otter out, that he might be shot while making his way across a few yards of stone and tangle to the sea.   I have known nine killed in this one den in a single year. But sometimes the otter occupied a den a few hundred yards inland, where a desperate fight ensued between him and the dogs. Long before the den was reached, the dogs became nervous and impatient, whining, and glancing up to the face of their master, and, with anxious look, springing up and licking his hands.   To let them off until quite close to the den was sure to destroy the sport, as the otter would, on hearing them bark, make at once for the sea.   Gasgach could, without difficulty, be kept in the rear, but little Cuilag, conscious of her moral weakness to resist temptation, begged to be carried.

Though she made no struggle to escape, yet
she trembled with eagerness, as, with cocked
ears and low cry, she looked out for the spot
where she and Gasgach would be set at liberty.
That spot reached—what a hurry-scurry, as
off they rushed to the den, and sprang in !
Gasgach's short bark was a certain sign that
the enemy was there; it was the first shot
in the battle. If Cuilag followed, the battle
had begun. One of the last great battles
fought by Cuilag was in that inland den.
On gazing down between two rocks which
below met at an angle, there, amidst fierce
barkings and the muffled sound of a fierce
combat; Cuilag's head and the head of a
huge otter, were seen alternately appearing,
as the one tried to seize the throat, and the
other to inflict a wound on his little antago-
nist. At last Cuilag made a spring, and
seized hold of the otter about the nose or lip.
A shepherd who was present, fearing the
dog would be cut to pieces, since the den
was too narrow to admit Gasgach (who
seemed half apoplectic with passion and ina-

bility to force his way in), managed, by a
great effort, to get hold of the otter's tail,
and to drag him upwards through a hole
like a chimney. The shepherd was terrified
that the otter, when it got its head out,
would turn upon him and bite him,—and
such a bite as those beautiful teeth can give!
—but to his astonishment, the brute
appeared with Cuilag hanging to the upper
lip. Both being flung on the grass, Gasgach
came to the rescue, and very soon, with
some aid from the boys, the animal of fish
and fur was killed and brought in triumph
to the manse.

There is a true story about Cuilag which
is worth recording. The minister, accompanied by Cuilag, went to visit a friend, who
lived sixty miles off in a direct line from the
manse. To reach him he had to cross several wild hills, and five arms of the sea or
freshwater lochs stretching for miles. The
dog, on arriving at her destination, took her
place, according to custom, on the friend's
hearthrug, from which, however, she was

ignominiously driven by a servant, and sent
to the kitchen. She disappeared, and left
no trace of her whereabouts. One evening,
about a fortnight afterwards, little Cuilag
entered the manse parlor, worn down to
a skeleton, her paws cut and swollen, and
she hardly able to crawl to her master, or
to express her joy at meeting all her dear
old friends once more. Strange to say, she
was accompanied into the room by Gasgach,
who, after frolicking about, seemed to apolo-
gize for the liberty he took, and bolted out
to bark over the glebe, and tell the other
dogs who had gathered round what had happened. How did Cuilag discover the way
home since she had never visited that part
of the country before? How did she go
round the right ends of the lochs, which had
been all crossed by boat on their journey,
and then recover her track, travelling twice
or thrice sixty miles? How did she live?
These were questions which no one could
answer, seeing Cuilag was silent. She
never, however, recovered that two weeks'

wilderness journey. Her speed was ever after less swift, and her gripe less firm.

The games of the boys were all athletic, —throwing the hammer, putting the stone, leaping, and the like. Perhaps the most favorite game was the "shinty," called *hocky*, I believe, in England. This is played by any number of persons, 100 often engag- in it. Each has a stick bent at the end, and made short or long, as it is to be used by one or both hands. The largest and smoothest field that can be found is selected for the game. The combat lies in the at- tempt of each party to knock a small wooden ball beyond a certain boundary in his oppo- nent's ground. The ball is struck by any one on either side who can get at it. Few games are more exciting, or demand more physical exertion than a good shinty match.

I have said nothing regarding a matter of more importance than anything touched upon in this chapter, and that is the *relig- ious* education of the manse boys. But

there was nothing so peculiar about it as to
demand special notice. It was very real
and genuine; and perhaps its most distin-
guishing feature was, that instead of being
confined to " tasks," and hard, dry, starched
Sundays only, it was spread over all the
week, and consisted chiefly in developing the domestic affections by a frank, loving, sympathizing intercourse between parents and children; by making home happy
to the " bairns ;" by training them up wisely
and with *tact*, to reverence *truth*,—truth in
word, in deed, and manner ; and to practise
unselfishness and courteous considerateness
towards the wants and feelings of others.
These and many other minor lessons were
never separated from Jesus Christ, the
source of all life. They were taught to
know him as the Saviour, through whose
atonement their sins were pardoned, and
through whose grace alone, obtained daily
in prayer, they could be made like himself.
The teaching was *real*, and was felt by the
boys to be like sunshine on dew, warming,

refreshing, and quickening their young
hearts ; and not like a something forced into
the mind, with which it had no sympathy, as
a leaden ball is rammed down into a gun-
barrel. Once I heard an elderly Highland
gentleman say that the first impression he
ever received of the reality of religion was
in connexion with the first death which occurred among the manse boys.

Need I add, in conclusion, that the manse
was a perfect paradise for a boy during his
holidays ! Oh, let no anxious mother interfere at such times with loving grandmother
and loving aunts or uncles ! No doubt there
is a danger that the boy may be " spoilt."
In spite of the Latin or Greek lessons which
his grandpapa • or the tutor delights to
give him in the morning, his excellent
parents write to say that " too much idleness
may injure him." Not a bit ! The boy is
drinking in love with every drink of warm
milk given him by the Highland dairymaid,
and with every look, and kiss, and gentle
hug given him by his dear grannie or aunts.

Education, if it is worth anything, *draws out*
as much as it puts in ; and this sort of education will strengthen his brain and brace his
nerves for the work of the town grammar-
school, to which he must soon return. " It
does not do to pamper him too much, it may
make him selfish," also write his parents.
Quite true as an educational axiom ; but his
grandmother denies—bless her for it, dear,
good woman !—that giving him milk or
cream *ad libitum*, with " scones" and cheese
at all hours, is pampering him. And his
aunts take him on their knee, and fondle
him, and tell stories, and sit beside him when
he is in bed, and sing songs to him ; and
there is not a herd or shepherd but wishes
to make him happy ; and old Rory has him
always beside him in the boat, and gives him
the helm; and, in spite of the old hand holding the tiller behind the young one, per-
suades his " darling," as he calls him, that it is
he, the boy, who steers the boat. Oh ! sunshine of youth, let it shine on ! Let love
flow out fresh and full, unchecked by any

rule but what love creates; pour thyself
down without stint into the young heart;
make his days of boyhood happy, for other
days must come of labor and of sorrow,
when the memory of those dear eyes, and
clasping hands, and sweet caressings, will,
next to the love of God from whence they
flow, save the man from losing faith in the
human heart, help to deliver him from the
curse of selfishness, and be an Eden in his
memory, when driven forth into the wilderness of life!

IV.

The Manse Girls.

"Dost thou remember all those happy meetings
   In summer evenings round the open door;
Kind looks, kind words, and tender greetings
   From clasping hands, whose pulses beat no more—
Dost thou remember them?"

THE manse girls were many. They formed a large family, a numerous flock, a considerable congregation; or, as the minister expressed it in less exaggerated terms, "a heavy handful." One part of their education, as I have already noticed, was conducted by a governess. The said governess was the daughter of a "governor," or commandant of one of the Highland forts—whether Fort-Augustus or Fort-William I remember not—where he had for years reigned

over a dozen rusty guns, and half as many
soldiers, with all the dignity of a man who
was supposed to guard the great Southern
land against the outbreaks and incursions of
the wild Highland clans, although, in truth,
the said Highland clans had been long asleep
in the old kirkyard "amang the heather," for
as the song hath it,

> " No more we'll see such deeds again,
> Deserted is the Highland glen,
> And mossy cairns are o'er the men,
> Who fought and died for Charlie."

The " major "—for the commandant had
attained that rank in the first American war
—left an only daughter who was small and
dumpy in stature, had no money, and but
one leg.　Yet was she most richly provided
for otherwise with every womanly quality,
and the power of training girls in "all the
branches" then considered most useful for
sensible well-to-do women and wives. She
was not an outsider in the family, or a mere
teaching machine, used and valued like a mill

or plough for the work done, but a member
of the household, loved and respected for her
own sake. She was so dutiful and kind that
the beat of her wooden leg on the wooden
stair became musical—a very beating of time
with all that was best and happiest in her pupils' hearts. She remained for some time
educating the younger girls, until a batch of
boys broke the line of feminine succession,
and then she retired for a time to teach one
or more families in the neighborhood. But
no sooner was the equilibrium of the manse
restored by another set of girls, than the little governess returned to her old quarters,
and once more stumped through the school-
room, with her happy face, wise tongue, and
cunning hand.

The education of the manse girls was neither learned nor fashionable. They were
taught neither French nor German, music
nor drawing, while dancing as an art was out
of the question, with the wooden leg as the
only artist to teach it. The girls, however,
were excellent readers, writers, and arithme-

ticians; and they could sew, knit, shape
clothes, and patch to perfection. I need
hardly say that they were their own and
their mother's only dressmakers, and manifested wonderful skill and taste in making
old things look new, and in so changing the
cut and fashion of the purchases made long
ago from the packman, that Mary's "everlasting silk," or Jane's merino, seemed capable
of endless transformations; while their bon-
nets, by judicious turning, trimming, and
tasteful placing of a little bit of ribbon
looked always fresh and new.

Contrasted with an expensive and fashionable education, theirs will appear to have
been poor and vulgar. Yet in the long
course of years, I am not sure but the manse
girls had the best of it. For one often won
ders what becomes of all this fashionable education in the future life of the young lady.
What French or German books does she
read as a maid or matron? With whom
does she, or can she, converse in these languages? Where is her drawing beyond the

Madonna's heads and the Swiss landscape which she brought from school, touched up by the master? What music does she love and practise for the sake of its own beauty, and not for the sake of adding to the hum of the drawing-room after dinner? The manse girls could read and speak two languages, at least—Gaelic and English. They could sing, too, their own Highland ditties: wild, but yet as musical as mountain streams and summer winds; sweet and melodious as song of thrush or blackbird in spring, going right to the heart of the listener, and from his heart to his brimming eyes. And so I am ready to back the education of the poor manse against that of many a rich and fashionable mansion, not only as regards the ordinary "branches," but much more as developing the mental powers of the girls. At all events they acquired habits of reflective observation, with a capacity of thoroughly relishing books, enjoying Nature in all her varying scenes and moods, and of expressing their own thoughts and sentiments with such a freshness and force as made them most delightful members of society. A fashionable education, on the other hand, is often a mere tying on to a tree of a number of "branches" without life, instead of being a developing of the tree itself, so that it shall bear its own branches loaded with beautiful flowers and clustering fruit.

But the manse school included more rooms than the little attic where the girls met around that familiar knot of wood which projected from beneath the neat calico of the major's daughter. The cheerful society of the house; the love of kindred,— each heart being as a clear spring that sent forth its stream of affection with equable flow to refresh others; the innumerable requirements of the glebe and farm; the spinning and shearing; the work in the laundry, the kitchen, and the dairy; the glorious out-door exercise over field and moor, in the glens or by the shore; the ministrations of charity, not with its doled-out alms to beggars only, but with its "kind words and looks and tender greetings" to the many cottagers around,—these all were teachers in the Home School. And thus, partly from circumstances, partly, it must be acknowledged, from rare gifts of God bestowed upon them, they all grew up with a purity, a truthfulness, a love and gladness, which made the atmosphere of the manse one of constant sunshine. Each had her own strong individual character, like trees which grow free on the mountain side. They delighted in books, and read them with head and heart, undisturbed by the slang and one-sided judgments of hack critics. And it occasionally happened that some Southern friend, who in his wanderings through the Highlands enjoyed the hospitality of the manse, sent the girls a new volume of pleasant literature as a remembrance of his visit. These gifts were much valued, and read as volumes are seldom read now-a-days. Books of good poetry especially were so often conned by them that they became as portions of their own thoughts.

The manse girls did not look upon life as a vain show, aimless and purposeless ; upon everything and every person as " a bore ;" cr upon themselves as an insupportable burden to parents and to brothers,—unless they got husbands ! Choice wives they would have made, for both their minds and bodies had attractions not a few ; and " good offers," as they were called, came to them as to others. Young men had been "daft" about them, aud they were too sensible and womanly not to wish for a home they could call their own ; yet it never crossed their thoughts that they *must* marry, just as one must get a pair of shoes. They never imagined that it was possible for any girl of principle and feeling to marry a man whom she did not love, merely because he had a number of sheep and cattle in a Highland farm ; or had good prospects from selling tea and sugar in Glasgow , or had a parish as a minister, or a property as a "laird." Poor

foolish creatures were they not, to think so ?
without one farthing they could call their
own; with no prospects from their father, the
minister; with no possessions save what he
had last purchased for them from the packman ! What on earth would come of them
or of their mother if the parson was
drowned some stormy night with Ruari
and "the Roe ?" Were they to be cast on
the tender mercies of this or that brother
who had a home over their heads ? What ?
a brother to afford shelter to a sister ! Or
could they seriously intend to trust Providence for the future, if they only did His
will for the present ? Better far, surely, to
accept the first good offer; snatch at the
woolly hand of the large sheep-farmer, the
sweet hand of the rich grocer, the thin,
sermon-writing hand of the preacher; nay,
let them take their chance even with James,
the tutor, who has been sighing over each of
them in turn ! But no; like "fools," they
took for granted that it never could come
wrong in the end to do what was right at

the time, and so they never thought it to be absolutely incumbent on them to " marry for marrying sake." Neither father nor mother questioned the propriety of their conduct. And thus it came to pass that none of them, save one, who loved most heroically and most truly unto death, ever married. The others became what married ladies and young expectants of that life-climax call—Old Maids. But many a fire-side, and many a nephew and niece, with the children of a second generation, blessed God for them as precious gifts. . .

I feel that no apology is required for quoting the following extract from a letter written by the pastor, more than sixty years ago, when some of the eldest of the manse girls left home for the first time. It will find, I doubt not, a response in the heart of many a pastor in similar circumstances :—

" It was, my dear, my very dear girls, at seven in the morning of·Thursday, the 31st August, you took your departure from the old quay—that quay where I often landed

in foul and fair weather, at night and by
day ; my heart always jumping before me,
anticipating the happiness of joining the delightful group that formed my fireside,— a
group I may never see collected again.
How happy the parents, the fewest in number, who can have their families within their
reach ! happier still, when, like you, their
families are to them a delight and comfort !
You left the well-known shores of ——, and
your parents returned with heavy steps, the
weight of their thoughts making their ascent
to the manse much slower and harder to ac-
complish than ever they found it before.
We sat on the hill-side bathed in tears, giving many a kind and longing look to the
wherry, which always went further from us,
till our dim eyes, wearied of their exertions,
could see nothing in its true state ; when,
behold, cruel Castle Duart interrupted our
view, and took out of our sight the boat
that carried from us so much of our worldly
treasure.   Our thousand blessings be with
our dear ones, we cried, and returned to the

house,—to the manse of ——; a house
where much comfort and happiness were
always· to be found; where the friend was
friendly treated, and where the stranger
found himself· at home; where the distressed
and the needy met with pity and kindness,
and the beggar never went off without being
supplied; where the story and the joke often
cheered the well-pleased guests, and were
often accompanied with the dance and the
song, and all with an uncommon degree of
elegance, cheerfulness, and good humor.
But with me these wonted scenes of merriment are now over. The violin and the song
have no charms for me; and the cheerful
tale delights no more. But hold, minister!
what mean you by these gloomy thoughts?
Why disturb for a moment the happiness of
the dear things you write to, and for whose
happiness you so earnestly pray, by casting a
damp upon their gay and merry hours?
Cease, foolish, and tempt not Providence to
afflict you! What! have you not many comforts to make you happy? Is not the friend

of your bosom, the loving dutiful wife, and the loving dutiful mother, alive to bless and to comfort you? Is not your family, though somewhat scattered, all alive? Are they not all good and promising? None of them ever yet caused you to blush; and are not these great blessings? and are they not worthy of your most cheerful and grateful acknowledgements? They are, they are, and I bless God for the goodness. But the thought—I cannot provide for these! Take care, minister, that the anxiety of your affection does not unhinge that confidence with which the Christian ought to repose upon the wise and good providence of God! What though you are to leave your children poor and friendless? Is the arm of the Lord shortened that he cannot help? is his ear heavy that he cannot hear? You yourself have been no more than an instrument in the hand of his goodness; and is his goodness, pray, bound up in your feeble arm? Do you what you can; leave the rest to God. Let them be good, and fear the Lord, and

keep the commandants, and he will provide
for them in his own way and in his time.
Why then wilt thou be cast down, O my soul;
why disquieted within me? Trust thou in
the Lord! Under all the changes and the
cares and the troubles of this life, may the
consolations of religion support our spirits.
In the multitude of the thoughts within me,
thy comforts, O my God, delight my soul!
But no more of this preaching-like harangue,
of which, I doubt not, you wish to be
relieved. Let me rather reply to your letter,
and tell you my news."

It was after this period that he had to
mourn the loss of many of his family. And
then began for the manse-girls the education
within the school of sickness and death,
whose door is shut against the intrusion of
the noisy world, and into which no one can
enter, except the Father of all, and "the
Friend who sticketh closer than a brother."

The first break in a family is a solemn and
affecting era in its history; most of all when
that family is "all the world" to its own

members. The very thought—so natural to others who have suffered—that this one who has been visited by disease can ever become *dangerously* ill—can ever die, is by them dismissed as a dreadful night-mare. Then follow "the hopes and fears that kindle hope, an undistinguishable throng;" the watchings which turn night into day, and day into night; the sympathy of sorrow which makes each mourner hide from others the grief that in secret is breaking the heart; the intense realization, at last for all that may be—ay, that must be—until the last hours come, and what these are they alone know who have loved and lost. What a mighty change does this first death make in a family, when it is so united, that if one member suffers all suffer! It changes everything. The old haunts by rock or stream can never be as they were; old songs are hushed for years, and, if ever sung again, they are like wails for the dead; every room in the house seems, for a time, tenanted more by the dead than by the living; the books are theirs;

in church is not empty, but occupied by
them; plans and purposes, family arrangements and prospects, all seem for a time so
purposeless and useless. No one ever calculated on this possibility! The trial which
has come verily seems "strange." Yet this
is, under God, a holy and blessed education.
Lessons are then taught, "though as by
fire," which train all the scholars for a
higher school. And if that old joyousness
and hilarity pass away which belong to a
world that seemed as if it could not change
—like a very Eden before the fall—it is succeeded by a deeper life; a life of faith and
hope which find their rest in the unchanging
rather than the changing present.

Such was a portion of the education which
the pastor and his family received for many
succeeding years in the old manse; but its
memory was ever accompanied by thanksgiving for the true, genuine Christian life
and death of those who had died. I need
hardly say that the girls, more than the other
members of the family, shared these sorrows

and this discipline; for whatever men can do in the storm of ocean or of battle, women are the ministering angels in the room of sickness and of suffering.

Before I turn away from the manse girls, I must say something more of their little governess. She lingered long about the manse, as a valued friend, when her services were no longer needed. But she resolved at last to attempt a school in the low country, and to stamp some uneducated spot with the impress of the wooden knob. Ere doing so, she confided to the minister a story told her by her father, the fort-commandant, about some link or other which bound him to the Argyle family. What that link precisely was, no history records. It may have been that her mother was a Campbell, or that the major had served in a regiment commanded by some member of that noble house, or had picked an Argyle out of the trenches of Ticonderoga. Anyhow, the commandant fancied that his only daughter would find a crutch of support, like many others, in " the

Duke," if he only knew the story. Never up to this time was the crutch needed; but needed it is now if she is to pursue her life-journey in peace. Why not tell the story then to the Duke? quoth the minister. Why not? thoughtfully ruminated the little governess. And so they both entered the manse-study—a wonderful little sanctum of books and MSS., with a stuffed otter and wild-cat, a gun, compass, coil of new rope, the flag of the "Roe," a print of the Duke of Argyle, and of several old divines and reformers, in wigs and ruffs. There the minister wrote out, with great care, a petition to the Duke for one of the very many kind charities, in the form of small annuities, which were dispensed by his grace. The governess determined to present it in person at Inverary. But the journey thither was then a very serious matter. To travel now-a-days from London to any capital on the Continent is nothing to what that journey was. For it could only be done on horse-back, and by crossing several stormy ferries,

as wide as the Straits of Dover. The journey
was at last, however, arranged in this way.
There lived in one of the many cottages of
the glebe, a man called "old Archy," who
had been a servant in the family of the
pastor's father-in-law. Archy had long ago
accompanied, as guide and servant, the minister's wife, when she went to Edinburgh for
her education. Having been thus trained to
foreign travel, and his fame established as a
thoroughly-qualified *courier*, he was at once
selected to accompany, on horse-back, the
governess to Inverary. That excellent
woman did not, from nervous anxiety, go to
bed the night previous to her departure; and
she had labored for a fortnight to produce a
new dress in which to appear worthily before
the Duke. She had daily practised, moreover, the proper mode of address, and was
miserable from the conviction that all would
be ruined by her saying "Sir," instead of
"your Grace." The minister tried to laugh
her out of her fears, and to cheer her by the
assurance that a better-hearted gentleman

lived not than the good Duke John; and
that she must speak to him as she felt. She
departed with her black trunk slung behind
Archy; and also with extraordinary supplies
of cold fowls, mutton, ham, and cheese—not
to speak of letters commendatory to every
manse on the road. What farewells, and
kissings, and waving of handkerchiefs, and
drying of eyes, and gathering of servants and
of dogs at the manse-door, as the governess
rode off on the white horse, Archy following
on the brown! The proper arrangement of
the wooden leg had been a great mechanical
and æsthetic difficulty, but somehow the girls
with a proper disposal of drapery, had made
the whole thing *apropos*.   Archy too, had
patched up a saddle of wonderful structure
for the occasion.

Time passed, and in a fortnight, to the joy
of the household, the white mare was seen
coming over the hill, with the brown following; and soon the governess was once more
in the arms of her friends, and the trunk in
those of Archy. Amidst a buzz of questions,

the story was soon told with much flutter and
some weeping—how she had met the Duke
near the castle; how she had presented her
petition, while she could not speak; how his
Grace had expressed his great regard for
" his minister;" and how next day, when she
called by appointment, he signified his intention of granting the annuity. "It is like
himself," was the minister's only remark,
while his eyes were fuller than usual as he
congratulated the little governess on her
success ; and gave many a compliment to old
Archy for the manner in which he had
guided the horses and their riders. The
little governess taught her school for many
years, and enjoyed her annuity till near
ninety. During her last days, she experienced the personal kindness and tender
goodness of the present "Argyles," as she
had long ago done of the former "Argyles."

V.

The Minister and his Work.

"A genuine·priest,
The shepherd of his flock : or, as a king
Is styled, when most affectionately praised,
The father of his people. Such is he ;
And rich and poor, and young and old, rejoice
Under his spiritual sway."

WORDSWORTH.

IN Dr. Macculloch's " Tour to the Highlands
of Scotland," we have the most perfect
and eloquent descriptions of scenery·; but in
Dr. Johnson's, the truest yet most compli-
mentary delineations of the character and
manners of the people. The physical features of the country are, no doubt, abiding,
while its social condition is constantly
changing; so that we can now-a-days more
easily recognize the truth of the sketches by

the former than by the latter tourist. But
the minister of whom I write, and the manners of his time, belong to the era of
Johnson, and not to that of Macculloch.

There is something, by the way, peculiarly
touching in that same tour of the old
Doctor's, when we remember the tastes and
habits of the man, with the state of the
country at the time in which he visited it.
Unaccustomed to physical exercise, obese in
person, and short-sighted in vision, he rode
along execrable roads: and on a Highland
shelty cautiously felt his way across inter-
minable morasses. He had no means of
navigating those stormy seas but an open
boat, pulled by sturdy rowers, against wet-
ting spray, or tacking from morning till
night amidst squalls, rain, and turbulent
tideways. He had to put up in wretched pot-
houses, sleeping, as he did at Glenelg, "on a
bundle of hay, in his riding-coat; while Mr.
Boswell, being more delicate, laid himself in
sheets, with hay over and above him, and lay

in linen like a gentleman."   In some of the best houses, he found but clay floors below, and peet-reek around, and nowhere did he find the luxuries of his own favorite London. Yet he never growls or expresses one word of discontent or peevishness. Whether this was owing to his having for the first time escaped the conventionalities of city life ; or to the fact of the Highlands being then the last stronghold of Jacobinism; or to the honor and respect which was everywhere shown towards himself; or, what is more probable, to the genial influence of fresh air and exercise upon his phlegmatic constitution, banishing its " bad humors,"—in whatever way we may account for it, so it was, that he encountered every difficulty and discomfort with the greatest cheerfulness ; partook of the fare given him and the hospitality afforded to him with hearty gratitude ; and has written about every class of the people with the generous courtesy of a well-bred English gentleman.

His opinion of the Highland clergy is not

the least remarkable of his "testimonies,"
considering his intense love of Episcopacy,
and its forms of public worship, with his sincere dislike of Presbyterianism. "I saw," he
says, writing of the clergy, " not one in the
islands whom I had reason to think either
deficient in learning or irregular in life, but
found several with whom I could not converse without wishing, as my respect increased, that they had not been Presby-
terians." Moreover, in each of the distant
islands which the Doctor visited, he met
ministers with whom even he was able to
have genial and scholarly conversation.
"They had attained," he says, "a knowledge as may be justly admired in men who
have no motive to study but generous curiosity, or, what is still better, desire of use-
fulness; with such politeness as no measure
or circle of converse could ever have supplied,
but to minds naturally disposed to elegance."
When in Skye, he remarks of one of those
clergymen, Mr. M'Queen, who had been his

guide, that he was " courteous, candid, sensible, well informed, very learned;" and at parting, he said to him, "I shall ever retain a great regard for you. Do not forget me." In another island, the small island of Coll, he paid a visit to Mr. Maclean, who was living in a small, straw-thatched, mud-walled hut, "a fine old man," as the Doctor observed to Boswell, "well dressed, with as much dignity in his appearance as the Dean of a cathedral!" Mr. Maclean had "a valuable library," which he was obliged, "from want of accommodation, to keep in large chests;" and this solitary, shut up "in a green isle amidst the ocean's waves," argued with the awful Southern Don about Liebnitz, Bayle, etc., and though the Doctor displayed a little of the bear, owing to the old man's deafness, yet he acknowledged that he "liked his firmness and orthodoxy." In the island of Mull, again Johnson spent a night under the roof of another clergyman, whom he calls, by mistake, Mr. Maclean,

but whose name was Macleod,* and
of whom he says that he was "a minister
whose elegance of conversation, and strength
of judgment, would make him conspicuous
in places of greater celebrity." It is
pleasant to know, on such good authority,
that there lived at that time, in these wild
and distant parts, ministers of such character,
manners, and learning.

The minister of our Highland parish was a
man of similar culture and character with
those of his brethren, two of whom mentioned by the Doctor were his intimate friends.
He had the good fortune, let me mention in
passing, to meet the famous traveller at
Dunvegan Castle; and he used to tell, with
great glee, how he found him alone in the
drawing room before dinner, poring over
some volume on the sofa, and how the Doc-

---

* The grandfather of the present, and the father of
the late Rev. Dr. Macleod of New York, U. S., both
distinguished clergymen.

tor, before rising to greet him kindly, dashed to the ground the book he had been reading, exclaiming, in a loud and angry voice, " The author is an ass !"

When the minister came to his parish, the people were -but emerging from those old feudal times of clanship, with its loyal feelings and friendships, yet with its violent prejudices and intense clinging to the past, and to all that was bad as well as good in it. Many of his parishioners had been " out in the '45," and were Prince Charlie men to the core. The minister himself was a keen " Hanoverian." This was caused by his very decided Protestantism, and also, no doubt, by his devotion to the Dunvegan family, which, through the influence chiefly of President Forbes, had opposed the Pretender. The minister, on a memorable occasion, had his Highland and loyal feeling rather severely tried. It happened thus :— When King William IV., like our noble Prince Alfred, was a midshipman in the royal navy, his ship, the " Cæsar," visited

the Western Isles.   The minister, along with
the other public men in the district, went to
pay his respects to his Royal Highness.   He
was most graciously received, and while
conversing with the prince on the quarter-
deck, a galley manned with six rowers
pulled alongside.   The prince asked him to
whom it belonged.   On being informed that
it belonged to a neighboring proprietor, the
additional remark was made, with a kind
smile, " He was out, no doubt, in the '45 ?
Of course he was !   Ah, Doctor, all you
Highlanders were rebels, every one of you !
Ha—ha—ha !"   " Please your Royal Highness," said the minister, with a low bow, " I
am thankful to say *all* the Highlanders were
not rebels, for had they been so, we might
not have had the honor and happiness of
seeing your Royal Highness among us now."
The prince laughed heartily, and com-
plimented the minister on the felicity of his
reply.   These were not characterized by
much religion.   The predecessor of our minister had been commanded by this party

not to dare in their hearing to pray for King George in church, or they would shoot him dead. He did, nevertheless, pray, at least in words, but not, we fear, in pure faith. He took a brace of pistols with him to the pulpit, and cocking them before his prayer began, he laid them down before him, and for once at least offered up his petitions with his eyes open. There was no law-officer of the crown, not even a justice of the peace at that time in the whole parish. The people were therefore obliged to take the law to some extent in their own hands. Shortly after our minister came to the parish, he wrote stating that "no fewer than thirty persons have been expelled for theft, not by sentence of the magistrate, but by the united efforts of the better sort of the inhabitants. The good effects of this expulsion have been sensibly felt, but a court of law having been established since then in the neighborhood, the necessity for such violent means is in a great measure obviated."

The minister was too far removed from

the big world of Church politics, General
Assembly debates, controversial meetings
and pamphlets, to be a party man. It satis-
fied him to be a *part* of the great catholic
Church, and of that small section of it in
which he had been born. The business of
this Presbytery was chiefly local, and his
work was confined wholly to his parish.

After having studied eight years at a university, he entered on his charge with a
salary of £40, which was afterwards raised
to £80. He ministered to 2000 souls, all of
whom—with the exception of perhaps a
dozen families of Episcopalians and Roman
Catholics—acknowledged him as their pastor.
His charge was scattered over 130 square
miles, with a sea-board of 100! This is his
own description of the ecclesiastical edifices
of the parish at the beginning of his ministry:—"There are two churches *so called*,
but with respect to decency of accommodation, they might as properly be called sheds or
barns. The dimensions of each are no more
than forty by sixteen feet, and without seats

or bells. It is much to be regretted that since the Reformation little or no attention has been paid to the seating of churches in this country." No such churches can now be found. How the congregation managed to arrange themselves during service in those "sheds," I know not. Did they stand? sit on stones or bunches of heather? or recline on the earthen floor? Fortunately the minister was an eloquent and earnest preacher, and he may have made them forget their discomfort. But the picture is not pleasing of a congregation dripping wet, huddled together in a shed, without seats, after a long walk across the mountains: Sleeping, at all events, was impossible.

It is worth noticing, as characteristic of the time, that during the first period of his ministry there was no copy of the Gaelic Scriptures in existence, except the Irish Bible by Bedell. The clergy translated what they read to the people from the English version. The Highlanders owed

much to Gaelic hymns composed by some of
their own poets, and also to metrical trans-
lations of the psalms.   But even if there
had been Bibles, most of the people had not
the means of education.   What could one or
two schools avail in so extensive a parish?
To meet the wants of the people, a school
would require to be in almost every glen.

But preaching on Sunday, even on a
stormy winter's day, was the easiest of the
minister's duties.   There was not a road in
the parish.   Along the coast indeed for a
few miles there was what was charitably
called a road, and, as compared with those
slender sheep-tracks which wormed their
way through the glens, and across some of
the wilder passes, it perhaps deserved the
name.   By this said road country carts
could toil, pitching, jolting, tossing, in deep
ruts, over stones, and through the burns,
like waggons in South Africa, and with all
the irregular motion of boats in a storm.
But for twenty miles inland the hills and
glens were as the Danes had left them.

The paths which traversed those wilds were journeyed generally on foot, but in some instances by "the minister's horse," one of those sagacious creatures which, with wonderful instinct, seemed to be able, as Ruari used to say, "to smell out the road" in darkness. It is hardly possible to convey a just impression, except to those acquainted with Highland distances and wildernesses, of what the ordinary labors of such a minister were. Let us select one day out of many of a Highland pastor's work. Immediately after service, a Highlander saluted him with bonnet off and low bow, saying, "John Macdonald in the Black glen is dying, and would like to see you, sir." After some inquiry, and telling his wife not to be anxious if he was late in returning home, he strode off at "a killing pace" to see his parishioner. The hut was distant sixteen Highland miles; but what miles! Not such as are travelled by the Lowland or Southern parson, with steps solemn and regular, as if prescribed by law. But

this journey was over bogs, along rough
paths, across rapid streams without bridges,
and where there was no better shelter than
could be found in a Swiss châlet.   After
a long and patient pastoral visit to his
dying parishioner, the minister strikes for
home across the hills.   But he is soon met
by a shepherd, who tells him of a sudden
death which had occurred but a few hours
before in a hamlet not far off; and to
visit the afflicted widow will take him only a
few miles out of his course.   So be it, quoth
the parson, and he forthwith proceeds to the
other glen, and mingles his prayers with
the widow and her children.   But the
longest day must have an end, and the last
rays of the sun are gilding the mountain-
tops, and leaving the valleys in darkness.
And so our minister, with less elastic step,
is ascending toward the steep *Col*, which
rises for two thousand feet with great abrupt-
ness, and narrow zig-zag path from a chain
of lakes up past the " Rhigi " I have already
described.   But as he nears the summit,

down comes thick, palpable, impenetrable mist. He is confident that he knows the road nearly as well as the white horse, and so he proceeds with great caution over deep moor-hags until he is lost in utter bewilderment. Well, he has before now spent the night under a rock, and waited until break of day. But having eaten only a little bread and cheese since morning, he longs for home. The moon is out, but the light only reveals driving mist, and the mountain begins to feel cold, damp, and terribly lonely. He walks on, feeling his way with his staff, when suddenly the mist clears off, and he finds himself on the slope of a precipice. Throwing himself on his back on the ground, and digging his feet into the soil, he recovers his footing, and with thanksgiving changes his course. Down comes the mist again, thick as before. He has reached a wood—where is he? Ah! he knows the wood right well, and he has passed through it a hundred times, so he tries to do so now, and in a few minutes has fallen down a bank

into a pool of 'water. But now he surely
has the track, and following it he reaches the
spot in the valley from which he had started
two hours before! He rouses a shepherd,
and "they journey together to a ferry by
which he can return home by a circuitous
route. The boat is there, but the tide is out,
for it ebbs far to seaward at this spot, and so
he has to wait patiently for the return of the
tide. The tide turns, taking its own time.to
do so; half wading, half rowing, they at last
cross the strait. It is now daybreak, and
the minister journeys homeward, and reaches
the manse about five in the morning.

Such land journeys were frequently
undertaken, with adventures more or less
trying, not merely to visit the sick, but for
every kind of parochial duty—sometimes to
baptize, and sometimes to marry. These
services were occasionally performed in most
primitive fashion at one of those green spots
among the hills. Corrie Borrodale, among
the old "shieldings," was a sort of half-way-
house between the opposite sides of the

parish.· . There, beside a clear-well, children have been baptized; and there, among the bonnie blooming heather, he has married the Highland shepherd to his bonnie 'blooming bride. There were also in different districts preaching and " catechising," as it was called. The catechising consisted in examining on the Church Catechism and Scriptures every parishioner who was disposed to attend the meeting, and all did so with few exceptions. This "exercise" was generally followed by preaching, both of course in the open air, and when weather permitted. And no sight could be more beautiful than that of the venerable minister seated on the side of a green and sheltered knoll, surrounded by the inhabitants of the neighboring hamlets, each, as his turn came, answering, or attempting to answer, the questions propounded with gravity and simplicity. A simple discourse followed from the same rural pulpit, to the simple but thoughtful and intelligent congregation. Most touching was it to hear the Psalms rise from among the moorland, dis-

turbing " the sleep that is among the lonely
hills ;" the pauses filled up by the piping of
the plover or some mountain bird, and by
the echoes of the streams and water-falls
from the rocky precipices. It was a
peasant's choir, rude and uncultivated by
art, but heard, I doubt not, with sympathy
by the mighty angels who sung their own
noblest song in the hearing of shepherds on
the hills of Bethlehem.

That minister's work was thus devoted
and unwearied for half a century. And
there is something peculiarly pleasing and
cheering to think of him and of others of the
same calling and character in every church,
who from year to year pursue their quiet
course of holy, self-denying labor, educating
the ignorant ; bringing life and blessing into
the homes of disease and poverty ; sharing
the burden of sorrow with the afflicted, the
widow, and the fatherless ; reproving and
admonishing, by life and word, the selfish
and ungodly ; and with a heart ever open to
all the fair humanities of our nature—a true

"divine," yet every inch a man! Such men, in one sense, have never been alone—for each could say with his Master, "I am not alone, for the Father is with me." Yet what knew or cared the great, bustling, religious world about them? Where were their public meetings, with reports, speeches, addresses, resolutions, or motions about their work? Where their committees and associations of ardent philanthropists, rich supporters, and zealous followers? Where their "religious" papers, so called, to parade them before the world, and to crown them with the laurels of puffs and leading articles? Alone, he, and thousands like him have labored, the very salt of the earth, the noblest of their race

VI.

Passing Away.

THE minister, when verging on fourscore, became blind. A son of the manse, his youngest, was, to his joy, appointed to be his assistant and successor in the ministry. I can not forget the last occasion on which "the old man eloquent" appeared in the pulpit. The Holy Communion was about to be dispensed, and, before parting for ever from his flock, he wished to address them once more. When he entered the pulpit he mistook the side for the front; but old Rory, who watched him with intense interest, was immediately near him, and seizing a trembling hand, placed it on the book-board, thus guiding his master into the right position for addressing the congregation. And then stood up that venerable man, a Saul in height among the people, with his pure white hair falling back from his ample forehead over his shoulders. Few, and loving, and earnest were the words he spoke, amidst the profound silence of a passionately devoted people, which was broken only by their low sobs, when he told them that they should see his face no more. Soon afterwards he died. The night of his death, sons and daughters were grouped around his bed, his wife on one side, old Rory on the other. His mind had been wandering during the day. At evening he sat up in bed; and one of his daughters, who supported his head, dropped a tear on his face. Rory rebuked her and wiped it off, for it is a Highland superstition that no tear should ever drop on the face of a good man dying— is it because it adds to the burden of dying, or is unworthy of the glorious hopes of living? Suddenly the minister stretched forth his hand, as if a child were before him, and said, " I baptize thee in the name of the Father, the Son, and the Holy Spirit," then falling back, he expired.   It seemed as if it were his own baptism as a child of glory.

. The widow did not long survive her husband.   She had, with the quiet strength and wisdom of love, nobly fulfilled her part as wife and mother.   But who can know what service a wife and mother is to a family save those who have had this staff to lean on, this pillow to rest on, this sun to shine on them, this best of friends to accompany them, until their earthly journey is over, or far advanced?

Her last years were spent in peace in the old manse, occupied then and now by her youngest son.   But she desired, ere she died, to see her first-born in his lowland manse far away, and with him and his children to connect the present with the past.   She accomplished her wishes, and left an impress on the young of the third generation which they have never lost during the thirty years that have passed since they saw her face and heard her voice.   Illness she had hardly ever known.   One morning a grandchild gently

opened her bedroom door with breakfast.
But hearing the low accents of prayer, she
quietly closed it again and retired. When
she came again, and tapped and entered, all
was still. The good woman seemed asleep in
peace—and so she was, but it was the sleep
of death. She was buried in the Highland
kirkyard, beside her husband and nine of her
children. There, with sweet young ones, of
another generation, who have since then
joined them from the same manse, they rest
until the resurrection morning, when all will
meet " in their several generations."

Old Rory next followed his beloved master. One evening, after weeks of illness, he
said to his wife, " Dress me in my best ; get
a cart ready ; I must go to the manse and bless
them all, and then die." His wife thought
at first that his strange and sudden wish was
the effect of delirium, and she was unwilling
to comply. But Rory gave the command in
a tone which was never heard except when,
at sea or on land, he meant to be obeyed.
Arrayed in his Sunday's best, the old man,

feeble, pale, and breathless, tottered into the
parlor of the manse, where the family were
soon around him, wondering, as if they had
seen a ghost, what had brought him there.
"I bless you all, my dear ones," he said,
"before I die." And, stretching out his
hands, he pronounced a patriarchal blessing,
and a short prayer for their welfare. Shaking hands with each, and kissing the hand of
his old and dear mistress, he departed. The
family group felt awe-struck—the whole
scene was so sudden, strange and solemn.
Next day, Rory was dead.

Old Jenny, the henwife, rapidly followed
Rory. Why mention her? Who but the
geese or the turkeys could miss her? But
there are, I doubt not, many of my readers
who can fully appreciate the loss of an old
servant who, like Jenny, for half a century,
has been a respected and valued member of
the family. She was associated with the
whole household of the manse. Neither she
nor any of these old domestics had ever been

mere *things*, but living persons with hearts
and heads, to whom every burden, every joy
of the family were known.   Not a child but
had been received into her _embrace on the
day of birth ; not one who had passed away
but had received her tears on the day of
death ; and they had all been decked by her
in their last as in their first garments.   The
official position she occupied as henwife had
been created for her in order chiefly to re-
lieve her feelings at the thought of her being
useless and a burden in her old age.   When
she died, it was discovered that the affectionate old creature had worn next her heart
and in order to be buried .with her, locks of
hair cut off in infancy from the children
whom she had nursed.   And here I must re-
late a pleasing incident connected with her.
Twenty years after her death, the younger
son of the manse, and its present possessor,
was deputed by his church to visit, along
with two of his brethren, the Presbyterian
congregations of North America.   When on
the borders of Lake Simcoe he was sent for

by an old Highland woman who could speak
her own language only, though she had left
her native hills very many years before. On
entering her log hut the old woman burst into a flood of tears, and, without uttering a
word, pointed to a silver brooch which
clasped the tartan shawl on her bosom. She
was Jenny's youngest sister, and the silver
brooch she wore, and which was immediately
recognised by the minister, had been presented to Jenny by the eldest son of the
manse, when at college, as a token of affection for his old nurse.

Nearly forty years after the old minister
had passed away, and so many of "the old
familiar faces" had followed him, the manse
boat, which in shape and rig was literally
descended from the famous "Roe," lay becalmed, on a beautiful summer evening, opposite the shore of the glebe. The many
gorgeous tints from the setting sun were reflected from the bosom of the calm sea.
Vessels, "like painted ships upon a painted

ocean," lay scattered along "the Sound," and floated double, ship and shadow. The hills on both sides rose pure and clear into the blue sky, revealing every rock and precipice, with heathery knoll or grassy Alp. Fish sometimes broke the smooth unrippled sea, "as of old the Curlews called." The boating party had gone out to enjoy the perfect repose of the evening, and allowed the boat to float with the tide. The conversation happened to turn on the manse and parish.

" I was blamed the other day," remarked the minister, who was one of the party, " for taking so much trouble in improving my glebe, and especially in beautifying it with trees and flowers, because, as my cautious friend remarked, I should remember that I was only a life-renter. But I asked my adviser how many proprietors in the parish— whose families are supposed to have a better security for their lands than the minister has for the glebe—have yet possessed their properties so long as our poor family has possessed

the glebe ? He was astonished, on consider-
ation, to discover that every property in the
parish had changed its owner, and some of
them several times, since I had succeeded
my father."

" And if we look back to the time since
our father became minister," remarked another of the party, " the changes have been
still more frequent. The only possessors of
their first home, in the whole parish, are the
family which had no ' possessions ' in it."

" And look," another said, " at those who
are in this boat. How many birds are here
out of the old nest !" And strange enough,
there were in that boat the eldest and youngest sons of the old minister, both born on
the glebe, and both doctors of divinity, who
had done good, and who had been honored
in their time. There were also in the boat
three ordained sons of those old sons born of
the manse, in all, five ministers descended
from the old minister. The crew was made
up of an elderly man, the son of " old Rory,"

and of a white-haired man, the son of " old
Archy," both born on the glebe.

But these clergy represented a few only of
the descendants of the old minister who were
enjoying the manifold blessings of life.
These facts are mentioned here in order to
connect such mercies with the anxiety expressed sixty years ago by the poor parson
himself in the letter to his girls, which I
have published.

One event more remains for me to record
connected with the old manse, and then the
silence of the hills in which that lonely home
reposes, will no more be broken by any word
of mine about its inhabitants, except as they
are necessarily associated with other reminiscences. It is narrated in the memoir lately
published of Professor Wilson, that when the
eldest son of our manse came to Glasgow
College, in the heyday of his youth, he was
the only one who could compete in athletic
exercises with the Professor, who was his
friend and fellow student. That physical

strength, acquired in his early days by the manly training of the sea and hills, sustained his body : while a spiritual strength, more noble still, sustained his soul, during a ministry, in three large and difficult parishes, which lasted, with constant labor, more than half a century, and until he was just about to enter on his eightieth year—the day of his funeral being the anniversary of his birth. He had married in early life the daughter of one of the most honorable of earth, who had, for upwards of forty years, with punctilious integrity, managed the estates of the Argyle family in the Western Highlands. Her father's house was opposite the old manse, and separated from it by the "Sound." This invested that inland sea which divided the two lovers, with a poetry that made " The Roe " and her perilous voyages a happy vision that accompanied the minister until his last hour. For three or four years he had retired from public life to rest from his labors, and in God's mercy to cultivate the passive more than the active virtues in the bosom of his

own family. But when disposed to sink into
the silent pensiveness and the physical depression which often attend old age, one to-
pic, next to the highest of all, never failed to
rouse him—like a dying eagle in its cage,
when it sees afar off the mountains on which
it tried its early flight—and that one was
converse about the old parish, of his father,
and of his youth. And thus it happened that
on the very last evening of his life he was
peculiarly cheerful, as he told some stories
of that long past—and among others a characteristic anecdote of old Rory. How naturally did the prayer of thanksgiving then
succeed the memories of those times of peace
and of early happiness!

That same night his first and last love—
the " better half," verily, of his early life,.
was awoke from her anxious slumbers near
him, by his complaint of pain. But she had
no time to rouse the household ere he, putting his arms round her neck, and breathing
the words " my darling " in her ear, he fell
asleep. He had for more than twenty-five

years ministered to an immense congregation of Highlanders in Glasgow, and his public funeral was remarkable, not chiefly for
the numbers who attended it, or the crowds
which followed it—for these things are common in such ceremonies—but for the sympathy and sorrow manifested by the feeble and
tottering Highland men and women, many of
whom were from the old parish, and who,
bathed in tears, struggled to keep up with
the hearse, in order to be near, until the last
possible moment, one for whom they had an
enthusiastic attachment. The Highland hills
and their people were to him a passion—and
for their good he had devoted all the energies
of his long life; and not in vain. His name
will not, I think, be lost in this generation—
wherever at least the Celtic language is spoken, and though this notice of him may have
no interest to the Southern reader, who may
not know nor care to know his name, yet
every Gael in the most distant colony who
reads these lines, will pardon me for writing
them. He belongs to them as they did to him.

VII.

Characteristics of the Highland Peasantry.

I KNOW little from personal observation about the Highlanders in the far North, or in the central districts of Scotland, but I am old enough to have very vivid reminiscences of those in the West; and of their character, manners and customs as these existed during that transition period which began after "the 45," but which has now almost entirely passed away with emigration, the decay of the "kelp" trade, the sale of so many old properties, and the introduction of large sheep farms, deer forests, and extensive shootings. I have conversed with a soldier —old John Shoemaker, he was called—who bore arms under Prince Charlie. On the day I met him, he had walked several miles, was hale and hearty though upwards of a hundred years old, and had no money save ten shillings which he always carried in his pocket to pay for his coffin. He conversed quite intelligently about the olden time with all its peculiarities. I have also known very many who were intimately acquainted with the " lairds" and men of those days, and who themselves imbibed all the impressions and views then prevalent as to the world in general, and the Highlands in particular.

The Highlanders whom the tourist meets with now-a-days are very unlike those I used to know, and who are now found only in some of the remote unvisited glens, like the remains of a broken up Indian nation on the outskirts of the American settlements. The porters who scramble for luggage on the quays of Oban, Inverary, Fort William, or Portree; the gillies who swarm around a shooting box, or even the more aristocratic keepers—that whole set, in short, who live by summer tourists or autumnal sportsmen—

are to tne real Highlander, in his secluded parish or glen, what a commissionaire in an hotel at Innspruck is to Hofer and his confederates.

The real Highland peasantry are, I hesitate not to affirm, by far the most intelligent in the world. I say this advisedly, after having compared them with those of many countries. Their good breeding must strike every one who is familiar with them. Let a Highland shepherd from the most remote glen be brought into the dining room of the laird, as is often done, and he will converse with ladies and gentlemen, partake of any hospitality which may be shown him with ease and grace, and never say or do anything *gauche* or offensive to the strictest propriety. This may arise in some degree from what really seems an instinct in the race, but more probably it comes from the familiar intercourse which, springing out of the old family and clan feeling, always subsists between the upper and lower classes. The Highland gentleman never meets the most humble pea-

sant whom he knows without chatting with
him as with an acquaintance, even shaking
hands with him ; and each man in the district, with all his belongings, ancestry and
descendants included, is familiarly known to
every other.   Yet this familiar intercourse
never causes the inferior at any time, or for
a single moment, to alter the dignified respectful manner which he recognises as due to
his superior.   They have an immense reverence for those whom they consider real gentlemen or those who belong to the good families, however distantly connected with them.
No members of the aristocracy can distin-
guish more sharply than they do between
genuine blood though allied with poverty,
and the want of it though allied with wealth.
Different ranks are defined with great care
in their vocabulary.   The chief is always
called lord, " the lord of Lochiel," " the lord
of Lochhuy."   The gentlemen tenants are
called " men," " the man " of such and such
a place.   The poorest " gentleman " who
labors with his own hands is addressed i-

more respectful language than his better-to-
do neighbor who belongs to their own ranks,
The one is addressed as " you," the other as
" thou ;" and should a property be bought
by some one who is not connected with the
old or good families, he may possess thousands, but he never commands the same reverence as the poor man who has yet " the
blood " in him.   The " pride and poverty" of
the Gael have passed into a proverb, and express a fact.

· They consider it essential to good manners
and propriety never to betray any weakness
or sense of fatigue, hunger or poverty. They
are great admirers in others of physical
strength and endurance, those qualities
which are most frequently demanded of
themselves.   When, for example, a number
of Highland servants sit down to dinner, it is
held as proper etiquette to conceal the slightest eagerness to begin to eat ; and the eat-
ing, when begun, is continued with apparent
indifference, the duty of the elder persons
being to. coax the younger, and especially

any strangers that are present, to resume operations after they have professed to have partaken sufficiently of the meal.· They always recognise liberal hospitality as essential to a gentleman, and have the greatest contempt for narrowness or meanness in this department of life.   Drunkenness is rarely indulged in as a solitary vice, but too extensively, I must admit, at fairs and other occasions—funerals not excepted—when many meet together from a distance with time on their hands and money in their pockets.

The dislike to make their wants known or to complain of poverty, was also characteristic of them before the poor law was introduced, or famine compelled them to become beggars upon the general public.   But even when the civilized world poured its treasures twenty years ago, into the Fund for the Relief of Highland destitution, the old people suffered deeply ere they accepted any help. I have known families who closed their windows to keep out the light, that their children might sleep on as if it were night, an not rise to find a home without food. I remember being present at the first distribution of meal in a distant part of the Highlands. A few old women had come some miles, from an inland glen, to receive a portion of the bounty. Their clothes were rags, but every rag was washed, and patched together as best might be. They sat apart for a time, but at last approached the circle assembled round the meal depot. I watched the countenances of the group as they conversed apparently on some momentous question. This I afterwards ascertained to be, which of them should go forward and speak for the others. One woman was at last selected, while the rest stepped back and hung their heads, concealing their eyes with their tartan plaids. The deputy slowly walked towards the rather large official committee, whose attention, when at last directed to her, made her pause. She then stripped her right arm bare, and holding up the miserable skeleton, burst into tears and sobbed like a child. Yet, during all these sad destitution.

times, there was not a policeman or soldier
in those districts. No food riot ever took
place, no robbery was attempted, no sheep
was ever stolen from the hills—and all this
though hundreds had only shell-fish, or
" dulse," gathered on the seashore to depend
upon.

The Highlander is assumed to be a lazy
animal, and. not over honest in his dealings
with strangers. I have no desire to be a
special pleader in his behalf, with all my national predilections in his favor. But I must
nevertheless dissent to some extent from
these sweeping generalisations. He is naturally impulsive and fond of excitement, and
certainly is wanting in the steady, persever-
ing effort which characterises his Southern
brother. But the circumstances of his country, his small " croft " and want of capital,
the bad land and hard weather, with the
small returns for his uncertain labor, have
tended to depress rather than to stimulate
him. One thing is certain, that when he is
removed to another clime and placed in more

5

favorable circumstances, he exhibits a perseverance and industry which make him rise very rapidly.

It must be confessed, however, that Highland honesty is sometimes very lax in its dealings with the Sassenach. The Highlander forms no exception, alas, to the tribe of guides, drivers, boatmen, all over Europe, who imagine that the tourist possesses unlimited means, and travels only to spend money. A friend of mine who had been so long in India that he lost the Highland accent, though not the language, reached a ferry on his journey home, and, concealing his knowledge of Gaelic, asked one of the Highland boatmen what his charge was. "I'll ask the maister," was his reply. The master being unable to speak English, this faithful mate acted as interpreter. "What will you take from this Englishman?" quoth the interpreter. "Ask the fellow ten shillings," was the reply of the honest master, the real fare being five shillings. "He says," explained the interpreter, "that he is sorry he cannot do it under twenty shillings, and that's cheap." Without saying anything, the offer was apparently accepted, but while sailing across my friend spoke in Gaelic, on which the interpreter sharply rebuked him in the same language. " I am ashamed of you," he said ; " I am indeed, for I see you are ashamed of your country ; och, och, to pretend to me that you were an Englishman ! You deserve to pay forty shillings, but the ferry is only five !" Such specimens, however, are found only along the great tourist thoroughfares, where they are in every country too common.

I have said that the Highlanders are an intelligent, cultivated people, as contrasted with that dull, stupid, prosaic, incurious condition of mind which characterises so many of the peasantry in other countries. Time never hangs heavily on their hands during even the long winter evenings when outdoor labor is impossible. When I was young, I was sent to live among the peasantry " in the parish," so as to acquire a knowledge of the

language; and living, as I did, very much
like themselves, it was my delight to spend
the long evenings in their huts hearing their
tales and songs. These huts were of the most
primitive description. They were built of
loose stones and clay, the walls were thick,
the door low, the rooms numbered one only,
or in more aristocratic cases two. The floor
was clay, the peat fire was built in the middle of the floor, and the smoke, when amiable and not bullied by a sulky wind, escaped
quietly and patiently through a hole in the
roof. The window was like a porthole, part
of it generally filled with glass and part with
peat. One bed, or sometimes two, with clean
home-made sheets, blankets and counterpane
—a " dresser," with bowls and plates, a large
chest, and a corner full of peat, filled up the
space beyond the circle about the fire. Upon
the rafters above, black as ebony from peat
reek, a row of hens and chickens with a stately cock roosted in a Paradise of heat.

Let me describe one of these evenings.
Round the fire are seated, some on stools,

some on stones, some on the floor, a happy
group. Two or three girls, fine, healthy blue
eyed lasses, with their hair tied up with ribbon snood, are knitting stockings. Hugh,
the son of Sandy, is busking hooks ; big Archy is peeling willow wands and fashioning
them into baskets ; the shepherd Donald, the
son of Black John, is playing on the Jews'
harp ; while beyond the circle are one or
two herd boys in kilts, reclining on the floor,
all eyes and ears for the stories. The per-
formances of Donald begin the evening, and
form interludes to its songs, tales, and recit-
ations. He has two large "Lochaber
trumps," for Lochaber trumps were to the
Highlands what Cremona violins have been
to musical Europe. He secures the end of
each with his teeth, and grasping them with
his hands so that the tiny instruments are
invisible, he applies the little finger of each
hand to their vibrating steel tongues. He
modulates their tones with his breath, and
brings out of them Highland reels, strathspeys, and jigs—such wonderfully beautiful,

silvery, distinct and harmonious sounds as
would draw forth cheers and an encore even
in St. James's Hall. But Donald the son of
Black John is done, and he looks to bonny ·
Mary Cameron for a blink of her hazel eye to
reward him, while in virtue of his perform-
ance he demands a song from her. Now
Mary has dozens of songs, so has Kirsty, so
has Flory—love songs. shearing songs, wash-
ing songs, Prince Charlie songs, songs composed by this or that poet in the parish, and
therefore Mary asks, What song? So until
she can make up her mind, and have a little
playful flirtation with Donald the son of
Black John, she requests Hugh the son of
Sandy to tell a story. Although Hugh has
abundance of this material, he too protests
that he has none. But having betrayed this
n odesty, he starts off with one of those tales,
t! e truest and most authentic specimens of
v hich are given by Mr. Campbell, to whose
a 'mirable and truthful volumes I refer the
r ader.

When the story is done, improvisatore is

often tried, and amidst roars of laughter the
aptest verses are made, sometimes in clever
satire, sometimes with knowing allusions to
the weaknesses or predilections of those
round the fire. Then follow riddles and
puzzles ; then the trumps resume their tunes,
and Mary sings her song, and Kirsty and
Flory theirs, and all join in the chorus, and
who cares for the wind outside or the peat
reek inside ! Never was a more innocent or
happy group.

This fondness for music from trump, fiddle, or bagpipe, and for song singing, story
telling, and improvisatore, was universal, and
imparted a marvellous buoyancy and intelli-
gence to the people.

These peasants were, moreover, singularly
inquisitive, and greedy of information. It
was a great thing if the schoolmaster or any
one else was present who could tell them
about other people and other places. I remember an old shepherd who questioned me
closely how the hills and rocks were formed,
as a gamekeeper had heard some sportsmen

talking about this. The questions which are put are no doubt often odd enough. A woman, for example, whose husband was anxious to emigrate to Australia, stoutly opposed the step until she could get her doubt solved on some geographical point which greatly disturbed her. She consulted the minister, and the tremendous question which chiefly weighed on her mind was, whether it was true that the feet of the people there were opposite to the feet of the people at home? and if so—what then?

There is one science the value of which it is very difficult to make a Highlander comprehend, and that is mineralogy. He connects botany with the art of healing; astronomy with guidance from the stars, or navigation; chemistry with dyeing, brewing, &c.; but " chopping bits off the rocks," as he calls it, this has always been a mystery. A shepherd, while smoking his cutty at a small Highland inn, was communicating to another in Gaelic his experience of " mad Englishmen," as he called them. " There was one,"

said the narrator, " who once gave me his
bag to carry to the inn by a short cut across
the hills, while he walked by another road. I
was wondering myself why it was so dread-
fully heavy, and when I got out of his sight
I was determined to see what was in it.   I
opened it, and what do you think it was ?
But I need not ask you to guess, for you
would never find out.   It was stones !"
" Stones !" exclaimed his companion, opening his eyes. " Stones !   Well, well—that
beats all I ever knew or heard of them. And
did you carry it ?"   " Carry it ? Do you
think I was as mad as himself ? No ! I emp-
tied them all out, but I filled the bag again
from the cairn near the house, and gave him
good measure for his money."

The schoolmaster has been abroad in the
Highlands during these latter years, and few
things are more interesting than the eagerness with which education has been received
by the people. When the first deputation
from the Church of Scotland visited the
Highlands and islands, in a government

cruiser put at their disposal, to inquire into
the state of education and for the-establishing
of schools in needy districts, most affecting
evidence was afforded by the poor people of
their appreciation of this great boon. In one
island where an additional school was promised, a body of the peasantry accompanied
the deputation to the shore, and bade them
farewell with expressions of the most tender
and touching gratitude ; and as long as they
were visible from the boat, every man was
seen standing with his head uncovered. In
another island where it was thought necessary to change the site of the school, a woman
strongly protested against the movement. In
her fervor she pointed to her girl and said,
" She and the like of her cannot walk many
miles to the new school, and it was from her
dear lips I first heard the words of the blessed Gospel read in our house ; for God's sake
don't take away the school." Her pleading
was successful. Old men in some cases went
to school to learn to read and write. One old
man, when dictating a letter to a neighbor,

got irritated at the manner in which his sentiments had been expressed by his amanuensis, " I'm done of this !" he at length exclaimed. " Why should I have my tongue in another man's mouth when I can learn to think for myself on paper ?   I'll go to the school and learn to write."   And he did so. A class in another school was attended by elderly people.   One of the boys in it, who was weeping bitterly, being asked the cause of his sorrow, ejaculated in sobs, "I trapped my grandfather, and he'll no let me up !" The boy was immediately below his grandfather in the class, and having "trapped" or corrected him in his reading, he claimed the right of getting above him, which the old man had resisted.

I may notice, for the information of those interested in the education of the Irish or Welsh speaking populations, that Gaelic is taught in all the Highland schools, and that the result has been an immediate demand for English. The education of the faculties, and the stimulus given to acquire information, demand a higher aliment than can be afforded by the medium of the Gaelic language alone.   But it is not my intention to discourse, in these light sketches, upon grave themes, requiring more space and time to do them justice than our pages can afford.

Another characteristic feature of the Highland peasantry is the devoted and unselfish attachment which they retain through life to any of their old friends and neighbors.   An intimate knowledge of the families of the district is what we might expect.   They are acquainted with all their ramifications by blood or by marriage, and from constant personal inquiries, keep up, as far as possible, a knowledge of their history, though they may have left the country for years.   I marked, last summer, in the Highlands, the surprise of a general officer from India, who was revisiting the scenes of his youth, as old men, who came to pay their respects to him, inquired about every member of his family, showing a thorough knowledge of all the marriages which had taken place, and the

very names of the children who had been
born. " I declare," remarked the general,
that this is the only country where they care
to know. a man's father or grandfather !
What an unselfish interest, after all, do these
people take in one, and in all that belongs to
him. And how have they found all this out
about my nephews and nieces, with their
children ?" Their love of kindred, down to
those in whom a drop of their blood can be
traced, is not so remarkable, however, as this
undying interest in old friends, whether they
be rich or poor. Even the bond of a common
name—however absurd this appears—has its
influence still in the Highlands. I remember
when it was so powerful among old people,
as to create not only strong predilections,
but equally strong antipathies, toward strangers of whom nothing was known save their
name. This is feudalism fossilised. In the
Highlands there are other connections which
are considered closely allied to those of blood.
The connection, for instance, between children—it may be of the laird and of the peas-

ant—who are reared by the same nurse, is
one of these. Many an officer has been accompanied by his foster-brother to the wars,
and has ever found him his faithful servant
and friend unto death. Such an one was
Ewen McMillan who followed Col. Cameron,
as Fassiefern—as he was called, Highland
fashion, from his place of residence—to whom
Sir Walter Scott alludes in the lines—

" Proud Ben Nevis views with awe
How at the bloody Quatre Bas
Brave Cameron heard the wild hurrah
Of conquest as he fell."

The foster-brother was ever beside his dear
master, with all the enthusiastic attachment
and devotion of the old feudal times,
throughout the Peninsular campaign, until
his death. The 92nd Regiment was commanded by Fassiefern, and speaking of its
conduct at the Nile, Napier says, " How
gloriously did that regiment come forth to
the charge with their colors flying, and their
national music as if going to review ! This

was to understand war. The man (Colonel Cameron) who at that moment, and immediately after a repulse, thought of such military pomp, was by nature a soldier." Four days after this, though on each of those days the fighting was continued and severe, the 92nd was vigorously attacked at St. Pierre. Fassiefern's horse was shot under him, and he was so entangled by the fall as to be utterly unable to resist a French soldier, who would have transfixed him but for the fact that the foster-brother transfixed the Frenchman. Liberating his master, and accompanying him to his regiment, the foster-brother returned under a heavy fire and amidst a fierce combat to the dead horse. Cutting the girths of the saddle and raising it on his shoulders, he rejoined the 92nd with the trophy, exclaiming, " We must leave them the carcase, but they will never get the saddle on which Fassiefern sat." The Gaelic sayings " Kindred to twenty degrees, fosterage to a hundred," and " Woe to the father of the foster son who is unfaithful to his trust,"

were fully verified in McMillan's case.   I
may add one word about Colonel Cameron's
death as illustrative of the old Highland spirit.   He was killed in charging the French
at Quatre Bas.   The moment he fell, his foster-brother was by his side, carried him out
of the field of battle, procured a cart, and sat
in it with his master's head resting on his
bosom.   They reached the village of Water-
loo, where McMillan laid him on the floor of
a deserted house by the wayside.   The dying
man asked how the day went, expressed a
hope that his beloved Highlanders had be-
haved well, and that his country would believe he had served her faithfully; and then
commanded a piper, who had by this time
joined them, to play a pibroch to him, and
thus bring near to him his home among the
hills far away.   Higher thoughts were not
wanting, but these could mingle in the heart
of the dying Highlander with " Lochaber no
more."   He was buried on the 17th by
McMillan and his old brave friend Captain
Gordon—who still survives to tell the story

—in the *Allée Verte*, on the Ghent road. The following year the faithful foster-brother returned and took the body back to Lochaber; and there it lies in peace beneath an obelisk which the traveller, as he enters the Caledonian Canal from the South, may see near a cluster of trees which shade the remains of the Lochiel family, of which Fassiefern was the younger branch.

It must, however, be frankly admitted that there is no man more easily offended, more *thin-skinned*, who cherishes longer the memory of an insult, or keeps up with more freshness a personal, family, or party feud, than the genuine Highlander. Woe be to the man who offends his pride or vanity! " I may forgive, but I cannot forget," is a favorite saying. He will stand by a friend to the last, but let a breach be once made, and it is most difficult ever again to repair it as it once was. The grudge is immortal. There is no man who can fight and shake hands like the genuine Englishman.

It is difficult to pass any judgment on the

state of religion past or present in the Highlands. From the natural curiosity of the Highlanders, their desire to obtain instruction, the reading of the Bible, and the teaching of the Shorter Catechism in the schools, they are on the whole better informed in respect to religion than the poorer peasantry of other countries. But when their religious life is suddenly quickened it is apt to manifest itself for a time in enthusiasm or fanaticism, for the Highlander " moveth altogether if he move at all." The people have all a deep religious feeling, but that again, unless educated, has been often mingled with superstitions which have come down from heathen and Roman Catholic times. Of these superstitions, with some of their peculiar customs, I may have to speak in another chapter.

The men of " the 45 " were, as a class, half heathen, with strong sympathies for Romanism or Episcopacy, as the supposed symbol of loyalty. I mentioned in a former sketch how the parish minister of that time had prayed with his eyes open and his pistols cocked. But I have been since reminded of a fact which I had forgotten, that one of the Lairds who had " followed Prince Charlie," and who sat in the gallery opposite the parson, had threatened to shoot him if he dared to pray for King George, and, on the occasion referred to, had ostentatiously laid a pistol on the book-board. It was then only that the minister produced his brace to keep the Laird in countenance ! This same half-savage Laird was, in later years, made more civilised by the successor of the belligerent parson. Our parish minister, on one occasion, when travelling with the Laird, was obliged to sleep at night in the same room with him in a Highland inn. After retiring to bed, the Laird said, " O minister, I wish you would tell some tale." " I shall do so willingly," replied the minister; and he told the story of Joseph and his brethren. When it was finished, the Laird expressed his great delight at the narrative, and begged to know where the minister had picked it up, as it was evidently not Highland. "I got it," quoth the minister, "in a book you have often heard of, and where you may find other most delightful and instructive stories, which, unlike our Highland ones, are all true—in the Bible."

I will here record an anecdote of old Rory, illustrative of Highland superstition in its very mildest form. When "the minister" came to the parish, it was the custom for certain offenders to stand before the congregation during service, and do penance in a long canvas shirt drawn over their ordinary garments. He discontinued this severe practice, and the canvas shirt was hung up in his barn, where it became an object of awe and fear to the farm servants, as having somehow to do with the wicked one. The minister resolved to put it to some useful purpose, and what better could it be turned to than to repair the sail of the Roe, torn by a recent squall. Rory, on whom this task devolved, respectfully protested against patching the sail with the wicked shirt; but the more he

did so, the more the minister—who had himself almost a superstitious horror of superstition—resolved to show his contempt for
Rory's fears and warnings by commanding
the patch to be adjusted without delay, as he
had that evening to cross the stormy sound.
Rory dared not refuse, and his work was
satisfactorily finished, but he gave no response to his master's thanks and praises as
the sail was hoisted with a white circle above
the boom, marking the new piece in the old
garment.   As they proceeded on their voyage, the wind suddenly rose, until the boat
was staggering gunwale down with as much
as she could carry.   When passing athwart
the mouth of a wide glen which, like a fun-
nel, always gathered and discharged, in their
concentrated force, whatever squalls were
puffing and whistling round the hills, the sea
to windward gave token of a very heavy
blast, which was rapidly approaching the
Roe, with a huge line of foam before it, like
the white helmet crests of a line of cavalry
waving in the charge.   The minister was at

the helm, and was struck by the anxiety visible in Rory's face, for they had mastered many worse attacks in the same place without difficulty. "We must take in two reefs, Rory," he exclaimed, "as quickly as possible. Stand by the halyards, boys! quick and handy." But the squall was down upon them too sharp to admit of any preparation. "Reefs will do no good to-day," remarked Rory with a sigh. The water rushed along the gunwale, which was taking in more than was comfortable, while the spray was flying over the weather bow as the brave little craft, guided by the minister's hand, lay close to the wind as a knife. When the squall was at its worst, Rory could restrain himself no longer, but opening his large boat knife, sprang up and made a dash at the sail. Whirling the sharp blade round the white patch, and embracing a good allowance of cloth beyond to make his mark sure, he cut the wicked spot out. As it flew far to leeward like a sea bird, Rory resumed his seat, and wiping his forehead said, "Thanks to

Providence, that's gone! and just see how
the squall is gone with it." The squall had
indeed spent itself, while the boat was eased
by the big hole. " I told you how it would
be. Oh, never, never do the like again, minister, for it's a tempting of the devil." Rory
saw he was forgiven, as the minister and his
boys burst into a roar of merry laughter at
the scene.

One word regarding the attachment of the
Highlanders to their native country. "Characteristic of all savages," some reader may
exclaim; " they know no better." Now, I
did not say that the Highlanders knew no
better, for emigration has often been a very
passion with them as their only refuge from
starvation. Their love of country has been
counteracted on the one hand by the lash of
famine, and on the other by the attraction of
a better land opening up its arms to receive
them, with the promise of abundance to reward their toil. They have chosen, then, to
emigrate, but what agonising scenes have
been witnessed on their leaving their native

land ! The women have cast themselves on
the ground, kissing it with intense fervor.
The men, though not manifesting their attachment by such violent demonstrations on
this side of the Atlantic, have done so in a
still more impressive form in the Colonies,—
whether wisely or not is another question,—
by retaining their native language and cher-
ishing the warmest affection for the country
which they still fondly call " home." I have
met in British North America very many
who were born there, but who had no other
language than Gaelic. It is not a little re
markable that in South Carolina there are
about fifteen congregations in which Gaelic
is preached every Sunday, by native pastors,
to the descendants of those who emigrated
from their country about a century ago.

Among the emigrants from " the Parish,"
many years ago, was the piper of an old family which was broken up by the death of the
last Laird. Poor " Duncan Piper " had to
expatriate himself from the house which had
sheltered him and his ancestors. The even-

ing before he sailed he visited the tomb of
his old master, and played the family pibroch
while he slowly and solemnly paced round
the grave, his wild and wailing notes strange-
ly disturbing the silence of the lonely spot
where his chief lay interred.   Having done
so, he broke his pipes, and laying them on
the green sod. departed to return no more.

VIII.

The Widow and her Son.

A WIDOW, who was, I have heard, much loved for her " meek and quiet spirit," left her home in " the parish," early one morning, in order to reach before evening the residence of a kinsman who had promised to assist her to pay her rent. She carried on her back her only child. The mountain track which she pursued passes along the shore of a beautiful salt water loch, and then through a green valley watered by a peaceful stream, which flows from a neighboring lake. It afterwards winds along the margin of this solitary lake, until, near its further end, it suddenly turns into an extensive copse-wood of oak and birch. From this it emerges halfway up a rugged mountain side, and entering

a dark glen through which a torrent rushes
amidst great masses of granite, it conducts
the traveller at last, by a zigzag ascent, up
to a narrow gorge which is hemmed in upon
every side by giant precipices, with a strip of
blue sky overhead, all below being dark and
gloomy.

From this mountain-pass the widow's
dwelling was ten miles distant. She had
undertaken a long journey, but her rent was
some months overdue, and the sub-factor
threatened to dispossess her.

The morning on which she left her home
gave promise of a peaceful day. Before
noon, however, a sudden change took place
in the weather. Northward, the sky became
black and lowering. Masses of clouds came
down upon the hills. Sudden gusts of wind
began to whistle among the rocks, and to
ruffle with black squalls the surface of the
lake. The wind was succeeded by rain, and
the rain by sleet, and the sleet by a heavy
fall of snow. It was the month of May, and
that storm is yet remembered as the " great

May storm." The wildest day of winter never beheld snow-flakes falling faster, or whirling with more fury through the mountain-
pass, filling every hollow and whitening every rock.

Little anxiety about the widow was felt by
the villagers, as many ways were pointed out
by which they thought she could have escaped the fury of the storm. She might have
halted at the home of this farmer, or of that
shepherd, before it had become dangerous to
cross the hill. But early on the morning of
the succeeding day they were alarmed to
hear from a person who had come from the
place to which the widow was travelling,
that she had not made her appearance there.

In a short time about a dozen men mustered to search for the missing woman. They
heard with increasing fear at each house on
the track that she had been seen pursuing
her journey the day before. The shepherd
on the mountain could give no information
regarding her. Beyond his hut there was
no shelter—nothing but deep snow, and at

The Body of the Widow Found.

the summit of the pass, between the range
of rocks, the drift lay thickest.   There the
storm must have blown with a fierce and bitter blast.   It was by no means·an easy task
to examine the deep wreaths which filled up
every hollow.   At last a cry from one of the
searchers attracted the rest to a particular
spot, and there, crouched beneath a huge
granite boulder, they discovered the dead
body of the widow.

She was entombed by the snow.   A portion of a tartan cloak which appeared above
its surface led to her discovery.   But what
had become of the child ? Nay, what had
become of the widow's clothes, for all were
gone except the miserable tattered garment
which hardly concealed her nakedness!
That she had been murdered and stripped,
was the first conjecture suggested by the
strange discovery.   But in a country like
this, in which one murder only had occurred
in the memory of man, the notion was soon
dismissed from their thoughts.   She had
evidently died where she sat, bent

double ; but as yet all was mystery in regard to her boy or her clothing. Very soon however these mysteries were cleared up. A shepherd found the child alive in a sheltered nook in the rock, very near the spot where his mother sat cold and stiff in death. He lay in a bed of heather and fern, and round him were swathed all the clothes which the mother had stripped off herself to save her child. The story of her self-sacrificing love was easily read.

The incident has lived fresh in the memory of many in the parish ; and the old people who were present in the empty hut of the widow when her body was laid in it, never forgot the minister's address and prayers as he stood beside the dead. He was hardly able to speak from tears, as he endeavored to express his sense of that woman's worth and love, and to pray for her poor orphan boy.

More than fifty years passed away, when the eldest son of the manse, then old and grey headed, went to preach to his Highland congregation in Glasgow, on the Sunday pre-

vious to that on which the Lord's Supper
was to be dispensed. He found a compara-
tively small congregation assembled, for heavy snow was falling, and threatened to continue all day. Suddenly he recalled the story of the widow and her son, and this again
recalled to his memory the text, "He shall
be as the shadow of a great rock in a weary
land." He then resolved to address his people from these words, although he had carefully prepared a sermon on another subject.

In the course of his remarks he narrated
the circumstances of the death of the Highland widow, whom he had himself known in
his boyhood. And having done so, he asked,
"If that child is now alive, what would you
think of his heart, if he did not cherish an
affection for his mother's memory, and if the
sight of her clothes, which she had wrapped
round him in order to save his life at the cost
of her own, did not touch his heart, and even
fill him with gratitude and love too deep for
words? Yet what hearts have
hearers, if, over the memorials

viour's sacrifice of Himself, which you are to
witness next Sunday, you do not feel them
glow with deepest love, and with adoring
gratitude ?"

Some time after this, a message was sent
by a dying man, requesting to see the minister. The request was speedily complied with.
The sick man seized him by the hand, as he
seated himself beside the bed, and gazing in-
tently on his face, said, " You do not, you
cannot recognise me. But I know you, and
knew your father before you. I have been
a wanderer in many lands. I have visited
every quarter of the globe, and fought and
bled for my king and country. But while I
served my king I forgot my God. Though I
have been some years in this city, I never
entered a church. But the other Sunday, as
I was walking along the street, I happened
to pass your church door when a heavy
shower of snow came on, and I entered the
lobby for shelter, but not, I am ashamed to
say, with the intention of worshipping God,
or of hearing a sermon. But as I heard

them singing psalms, I went into a seat near
the door; then you preached; and then I
heard you tell the story of the widow and her
son,"—here the voice of the old soldier fal-
tered, his emotion almost choked his utter-
ance; but recovering himself for a moment,
he cried, "I am that son!" and burst into a
flood of tears. "Yes," he continued, "I am
that son! Never, never, did I forget my
mother's love. Well might you ask, what a
heart should mine have been if she had been
forgotten by me. Though I never saw her,
dear to me is her memory, and my only desire now is, to lay my bones besides hers in
the old churchyard among the hills. But,
sir, what breaks my heart and covers me
with shame is this—until now I never saw
the love of Christ in giving Himself for me,
a poor lost, hell-deserving sinner. I confess
it! I confess it!" he cried, looking up to
heaven, his eyes streaming with tears; then
pressing the minister's hand close to his
breast, he added, "It was God made you tell
that story. Praise be to His holy name that

6

my dear mother has not died in vain, and
that the prayers which, I was told, she used
to offer for me, have been at last answered;
for the love of my mother has been blessed
by the Holy Spirit for making me see, as I
never saw before, the love of the Saviour. I
see it, I believe it; I have found deliverance
now where I found it in my childhood,—in
the cleft of the rock; but it is the Rock of
Ages!" and clasping his hands he repeated
with intense fervor, " Can a mother forget
her sucking child, that she should not have
compassion on the son of her womb? She
may forget, yet will I not forget thee!"

He died in peace.

IX.

Tacksmen and Tenants.

THE " upper " and " lower " classes in the
Highlands were not separated from each
other by a wide gap. The thought was never
suggested of a great proprietor above, like a
leg of mutton on the top of a pole, and the
people far below, looking up to him with
envy. On reviewing the state of Highland
society, one was rather reminded of a pyra-
mid whose broad base was connected with
the summit by a series of regular steps. The
dukes or lords, indeed, were generally far removed from the inhabitants of the land, living as they did for the greater part of the
year in London ; but the minor chiefs, such
as " Lochnell," " Lochiel," " Coll," " Macleod," " Raasay," &c., resided on their res-

pective estates, and formed centres of local and personal influence. They had good family mansions, and in some instances the old keep was enlarged into a fine baronial castle, where all the hospitality of the far North was combined with the more refined domestic arrangements of the South. They had also their handsome barge, or well-built, well rigged smack or wherry; and their stately piper, who played pibrochs with very storms of sound after dinner, or, from the bow of the boat, with the tartan ribbands fluttering from the grand war-pipe, spread the news of the chief's arrival for miles across the water. They were looked up to and respected by the people. Their names were mingled with all the traditions of the country: they were as old as its history, practically as old, indeed, as the hills themselves. They mingled freely with the peasantry, spoke their language, shared their feelings, treated them with sympathy, kindness, and, except in outward circumstances, were in all respects, one of themselves. The poorest man on their estate

could converse with them at any time in the
frankest manner, as with friends whom they
could trust. There was between them an old
and firm attachment.

This feeling of clanship, this interest of the
clan in their chief, has lived down to my own
recollection. It is not many years—for I
heard the incident described by some of the
clan who took part in the *émeute*—since a
new family burial-ground was made in an old
property by a laird who knew little of the
manners or prejudices of the country, having
lived most of his time abroad. The first person whom he wished to bury in this new private tomb near "the big house," was his predecessor, whose lands and name he inherited
and who had been a true representative of
the old stock. But when the clan heard of
what they looked upon as an insult to their
late chief, they formed a conspiracy, seized
the body by force, and after guarding it for
a day or two, buried it with all honor in the
ancient family tomb on

" The Isle of Saints, where stands the old gray cross."

The Tacksmen at that time formed the most important and influential class of a society which has now wholly disappeared in most districts. In no country in the world was such a contrast presented as in the Highlands between the structure of the houses and the culture of their occupants. The houses were of the most primitive descrip tion, they consisted of one story—had only what the Scotch call a *but* and *ben ;* that is, a room at each end, with a court between, two garret rooms above, and in some cases a kitchen, built out at right angles behind. Most of them were thatched with straw or heather. Such was the architecture of the house in which Dr. Johnson lived with the elegant and accomplished Sir Allan Maclean, in the island of Inchkenneth. The old house of Glendessary, again, in " the Parish," was constructed, like a few more, of wicker-work, the outside being protected with turf, and the interior lined with wood. " The house and the furniture," writes Dr. Johnson, "were ever always nicely suited. We were

driven once, by missing our passage, to the
hut of a gentleman, when, after a very liberal supper, I was conducted to my chamber,
and found an elegant bed of Indian cotton,
spread with fine sheets. The accommodation
was flattering ; I undressed myself and found
my feet in the mire. The bed stood on the
cold earth, which a long course of rain had
softened to a puddle." But in these houses
were gentlemen, nevertheless, and ladies of
education and high breeding. Writing of
Sir Allan Maclean and his daughters, Johnson says, " Romance does not often exhibit a
scene that strikes the imagination more than
this little desert in these depths and western
obscurity, occupied, not by a gross herdsman
or amphibious fisherman, but by a gentleman
and two ladies of high rank, polished manners, and elegant conversation, who, in an
habitation raised not very far above the
ground, but furnished with unexpected neat-
ness and convenience, practised all the kindness of hospitality and the refinement of
courtesy." It was thus, too, with the old

wicker-house of Glendessary, which has not
left a trace behind. The interior was provided with all the comfort and taste of a modern mansion. The ladies were accomplished
musicians, the harp and piano sounded in
those " halls of Selma," and their descendants are now among England's aristocracy.

These gentlemen Tacksmen were generally
men of education ; they had all small but
well selected libraries, and had not only acquired some knowledge of the classics, but
were fond of keeping up their acquaintance
with them. It was not an uncommon pas-
time with them when they met together, to
try who could repeat the greatest number of
lines from Virgil or Horace, or who among
them, when one line was repeated, could *cap*
it with another line, commencing with the
same letter as that which ended the former.
All this may seem to many to have been pro-
fitless amusement, but it was not such amusement as rude and uncultivated boors would
have indulged in, nor was it such as is likely
to be imitated by the rich farmers who now

pasture their flocks where hardly a stone marks the site of those old homes.

I only know one surviving gentleman Tacksman belonging to the period of which I write, and he is ninety years of age, though in the full enjoyment of his bodily health and mental faculties. About forty years ago, when inspecting his cattle, he was accosted by a pedestrian with a knapsack on his back, who addressed him in a language which was intended for Gaelic. The Tacksman, judging him to be a foreigner, replied in French, which met no response but a shake of the head, the Tackman's French being probably as bad as the tourist's Gaelic. The Highlander then tried Latin, which kindled a smile of surprise, and drew forth an immediate reply. This was interrupted by the remark that English would probably be more convenient for both parties. The tourist, who turned out to be an Oxford student, laughing heartily at the interview, gladly accepted the invitation of the Tacksman to accompany him to his thatched home, and share his hospital-

ity. He was surprised on entering the room
to see a small library in the humble apartment. " Books here !" he exclaimed, as he
looked over the shelves. " Addison, Johnson, Goldsmith, Shakespeare—what ! Homer
too ?" The farmer, with some pride, begged
him to look at the Homer. It had been giv-
en as a prize to himself when he was a student at the University. My old friend will
smile as he reads these lines, and will wonder how I heard the story.

It was men like these who supplied the
Highlands with clergy, physicians, lawyers,
and the army and navy with many of their
officers. It is not a little remarkable that the
one island of Skye, for example, should have
sent forth from her wild shores since the beginning of the last wars of the French revo-
lution, twenty-one lieutenant-generals and
major-generals, forty-eight lieutenant-colo-
nels, six hundred commissioned officers, ten
thousand soldiers, four governors of colonies,
one governor-general, one adjutant-general,
one chief baron of England, and one judge of

the Supreme Court of Scotland. I remember
the names of sixty-one officers being enume-
rated, who during the war had joined the
army or navy from farms which were visible
from one hill-top in "the Parish." Those
times have now passed away. The Highlands furnish few soldiers or officers. Even
the educated clergy are becoming few.

One characteristic of these Tacksmen
which more than any other, forms a delightful reminiscence of them, was their remarkable kindness to the poor. There was hardly
a family which had not some man or woman
who had seen better days, for their guest,
during weeks, months, perhaps years. These
forlorn ones might have been very distant
relations, claiming that protection which a
drop of blood never claimed in vain; or former neighbors, or the children of those who
were neighbors long ago—or, as it often happened, they might have had no claim whatever upon the hospitable family, beyond the
fact that they were utterly destitute, yet
could not be treated as paupers, and had in

God's Providence been cast on the kindness
of others, like waves of the wild sea breaking
at their feet.   Nor was there anything very
interesting about such objects of charity.
One old gentleman beggar I remember, who
used to live with friends of mine for months,
was singularly stupid, often bad-tempered.
A decayed old gentlewoman, again, who was
an inmate for years in one house, was subject
to fits of great depression, and was by no
means entertaining.   Another needy visitor
used to be accompanied by a female servant.
When they departed after a sojourn of a few
weeks, the servant was generally laden with
wool, clothing, and a large allowance of tea
and sugar, contributed by the hostess for the
use of her mistress, who thus obtained supplies from different families during summer,
which kept herself and her red-haired domestic comfortable in their small hut during the
winter.   " Weel, weel," said the worthy
host, as he saw the pair depart, " it's a puir
situation that of a beggar's servant, like yon
woman carrying the bag and poke."   Now

this hospitality was never dispensed with a grudge, but with all tenderness and nicest delicacy.   These genteel beggars were received into the family, had comfortable quarters assigned to them in the house, partook of all the family meals, and the utmost care was taken by old and young that not one word should be uttered, nor anything done, which could for a moment suggest to them the idea that they were a trouble, a bore, an intrusion, or anything save the most welcome and honored guests.   This attention, according to the minutest details, was almost a religion with the old Highland gentleman and his family.

The poor of the parish, strictly so called, were, with few exceptions, wholly provided for by the Tacksmen.   Each farm, according to its size, had its old men, widows and orphans depending on it for their support.   The widow had her free house, which the farmers and the cottiers around him kept in constant repair.   They drove home from " the Moss " her peats for fuel—her cow had pasturage on the green hills. She had land sufficient to raise potatoes, and a small garden for vegetables. She had hens and ducks too, with the natural results of eggs, chickens, and ducklings. She had sheaves of corn supplied her, and these, along with her own gleanings were threshed at the mill with the Tacksman's crop. In short, she was tolerably comfortable, and very thankful, enjoying the feeling of being the object of true charity, which was returned by such labor as she could give, and by her hearty gratitude.

But all this was changed when those Tacksmen were swept away to make room for the large sheep farms, and when the remnants of the people flocked from their empty glens to occupy houses in wretched villages near the sea-shore, by way of becoming fishers—often where no fish could be caught. The result has been that "the Parish," for example, which once had a population of twenty-two hundred souls, and received only £11 per annum from public (Church) funds for the support of the poor, expends now

under the poor-law upwards of £600 annual-
ly, with a population diminished by one half,
and with poverty increased in a greater ra-
tio. This, by the way, is the result generally, when money awarded by law, and distri-
buted by officials, is substituted for the true
charity prompted by the heart and dispensed
systematically to known and well-ascertained
cases, that draw it forth by the law of sympathy and Christian duty. I am quite aware
of how poetical this doctrine is in the opinion of some political economists, but in these
days of heresy in regard to older and more
certain truths, it may be treated charitably.

The effect of the poor-law, I fear, has been
to destroy in a great measure the old feeling
of self-respect which felt it to be a degrada-
tion to receive any support from public charity when living, or to be buried by it when
dead. It has loosened also those kind bonds
of neighborhood, family relationship, and natural love which linked the needy to those
who could and ought to supply their wants,
and which was blessed both to the giver and

receiver. Those who ought on principle to support the poor are tempted to cast them on the rates, and thus to lose all the good derived from the exercise of Christian almsgiving. The poor themselves have become more needy and more greedy, and scramble for the miserable pittance which is given and received with equal heartlessness.

The temptation to create large sheep farms has no doubt been great. Rents are increased, and more easily collected. Outlays are fewer and less expensive than upon houses, &c. But should more rent be the highest, the noblest object of a proprietor? Are human beings to be treated like so many things used in manufactures? Are no sacrifices to be demanded for their good and happiness? Granting even, for the sake of argument, that profit, in the sense of obtaining more money, will be found in the long run to measure what is best for the people as well as for the landlord, yet may not the converse of this be equally true—that the good and happiness of the people will in the long run be

found the most profitable ? Proprietors, we
are glad to hear, are beginning to think that
if a middle-class tenantry, with small arable
farms of a rental of from twenty to a hundred
pounds per annum, were again introduced
into the Highlands, the result would be increased rents.   Better still, the huge glens,
along whose rich straths no sound is now
heard for twenty or thirty miles but the bleat
of sheep or the bark of dogs, would be tenanted, as of yore, with a comfortable and
happy peasantry.

In the meantime, emigration has been to a
large extent a blessing to the Highlands, and
to a larger extent still a blessing to the colonies.   It is the only relief for a poor and re-
dundant population.   The hopelessness of
improving their condition, which rendered
many in the Highlands listless and lazy, has
in the colonies given place to the hope of se-
curing a competency by prudence and industry.   These virtues have accordingly sprung
up, and the results have been comfort and
independence.   A wise political economy,

with sympathy for human feelings and attachments, will, we trust, be able more and more to adjust the balance between the demands of the old and new country, for the benefit both of proprietors and people. But I must return to the old tenants.

Below the "gentlemen" Tacksmen were those who paid a much lower rent, and who lived very comfortably, and shared hospitably with others the gifts which God gave them. I remember a group of men, tenants in a large glen which now "has not a smoke in it," as the Highlanders say, throughout its length of twenty miles. They had the custom of entertaining in rotation every traveller who cast himself on their hospitality. The host on the occasion was bound to summon his neighbors to the homely feast. It was my good fortune to be a guest when they received the present minister of "the Parish," while *en route* to visit some of his flock. We had a most sumptuous feast—oat-cake, crisp and fresh from the fire ; cream rich and thick, and more bountiful than nectar, what-

ever that may. be; blue Highland cheese,
finer than Stilton; fat hens, slowly cooked on
the fire in a pot of potatoes, without their
skins, and with fresh butter—"stoved hens,"
as the superb dish was called, and, though
last, not least, tender kid, roasted as nicely
as Charles Lamb's cracklin' pig. All was
served up with the utmost propriety on a table covered with a pure white cloth and with
all the requisites for a comfortable dinner, including the champagne of elastic, buoyant
and exciting mountain air. The manners
and conversation of those men would have
pleased the best-bred gentleman. Everything
was so simple, modest, unassuming, unaf-
fected, yet so frank and cordial. The conversation was such as might be heard at the
table of any intelligent man. Alas! there is
not a vestige remaining of their homes. I
know not whither they are gone, but they
have left no representatives behind. The
land in the glen is divided between sheep,
shepherds, and the shadows of the clouds.

There were annual festivals of the High-

land tenantry which deeply moved every
glen, and these were the Dumbarton and
Falkirk "Tysts," or fairs for cattle and sheep.
What preparations were made for these gatherings, on which the rent and income of
the year depended! What a collecting of
cattle, small and great, of drovers and of
dogs, the latter being the most interested
and excited of all who formed the caravan.
What speculations as to how the market
would turn out. What a shaking of hands
in boats, wayside inns, and on the decks of
steamers by the men in homespun cloth, gay
tartans, or in the more correct new garbs of
Glasgow or Edinburgh tailors, what a pouring in from all the glens increasing at every
ferry and village, and flowing on a river of
tenants and proprietors, small and great, to
the market! What that market was I know
not from personal observation, nor desire to
know.

> Let Yarrow be unseen, unknown,
>   If now we're sure to rue it,
> We have a vision of our own,
>   Ah, why should we undo it ?

The impression left in early years is too sublime to be tampered with. I have a vision of miles of tents, of flocks and herds surpassed only by those in the wilderness of Sinai; of armies of Highland sellers trying to get high prices out of the Englishmen, and Englishmen trying to get low prices out of the Highlandmen, but all in the way of "fair dealing."

When any person returned who had been himself at the market, who could recount its ups and downs, its sales and purchases, with all the skirmishes, stern encounters and great victories, it was an eventful. day in the Tacksman's dwelling. A stranger not initiated into the mysteries of a great fair might have supposed it possible for any one to give all information about it in a brief business form. But there was such an enjoyment in details, such a luxury in going over all the prices, and all that was asked by the seller and refused by the purchaser, and again asked by the seller, and again refused by the purchaser, with the nice financial fencing of

"splitting the difference," or giving back a
"luck's penny," as baffles all description. It
was not enough to give the prices of three-
year-olds and four-year-olds, yell cows, crock
ewes, stirks, stots, lambs, tups, wethers,
shots, bulls, &c., but the stock of each well-
known proprietor or breeder had to be dis-
cussed. Colonsay's bulls, Corrie's sheep,
Drumdriesaig's heifers, or Achadashenaig's
wethers, had all to be passed under careful
review. Then followed discussions about
distinguished beasts which had fetched high
prices, their horns, their hair, their houghs,
and general "fashion," with their parentage.
It did not suffice to tell that this or that great
purchaser from the south had given so much
for this or that lot, but his first offer, his remarks, his doubts, his advance of price, with
the sparring between him and the Highland
dealer, must all be particularly recorded, until the final shaking of hands closed the bar-
gain. And after all was gone over, it was a
pleasure to begin the same tune again with
variations. But who that has ever heard an

after-dinner talk in England about a good
day's hunting, or a good race, will be surprised at this endless talk about a market?

. I will close this chapter with a story told
of a great sheep farmer—not one of the old
gentleman tenants verily!—who, though he
could neither read nor write, had nevertheless. made a large fortune by sheep farming,
and was open to any degree of flattery as to
his abilities in this department of labor. A
purchaser, knowing his weakness, and anxious to ingratiate himself into his good gra-
ces, ventured one evening over their whisky
toddy to remark, " I am of opinion, sir, that
you are a greater man than even the Duke
of Wellington." " Hoot toot !" replied the
sheep farmer, modestly hanging his head
with a pleasing smile, and taking a large
pinch of snuff. " That is too much—too much
by far—by far." But his guest, after expa-
tiating for a while upon the great powers of
his host in collecting and concentrating upon
a Southern market a flock of sheep, suggested the question, " Could the Duke of Wel-

lington have done that ?"　The sheep farmer thought a little, snuffed, took a glass of toddy, and replied, "The Duke of Wellington was, no doot, a clever man ; very, very clever, I believe.　They tell me he was a good sojer, but then, d'ye see, he had reasonable men to deal with—captains, and majors, and generals that could understand him, every one of them, both officers and men ; but I'm not so sure after all if he could manage say twenty thousand sheep, besides black cattle, that could not undersand one word he said, Gaelic or English, and bring every hoof o' them to Fa'kirk Tryst.　I doot it—I doot it !　But *I* have often done that."　The inference was evident.

X.

Marriage of Mary Campbell.

MARY CAMPBELL was a servant in the old manse, about sixty years ago, and was an honest and bonny lassie. She had blue eyes and flaxen hair, with a form as "beautiful as the fleet roè on the mountain," a very Malvina to charm one of the heroes of old Ossian. Her sweetheart, however, was not an "Oscar of the spear," a "Cochullin of the car," or a Fingal who "sounded his shield in the halls of Selma," but was a fine-looking shepherd lad named Donald Maclean —who "wandered slowly as a cloud" over the hills at morning after his sheep, and sang his songs, played his trump, and lighted up Mary's face with his looks at evening. For two years they served together; and, as in

all such cases, these years seemed as a single
day. Yet no vows were exchanged, no en-
gagement made between them. Smiles and
looks, improvised songs full of lovers' *chaf-
fing*, joining together as partners in the
kitchen dance to Archy M'Intyre's fiddle,
showing a tendency to work at the same
hayrick, and to reap beside each other on
the same harvest rigs, and to walk home
together from the kirk—these were the only
significant signs of what was understood by
all, that bonny Mary and handsome Donald
were sweethearts.

It happened to them as to all lovers since
the world began ; the old history was repeated in the want of smoothness with which the
river of their affection flowed on its course.
It had the usual eddies and turns which belong to all such streams, and it had its little
falls, with tiny bubbles, that soon broke and
disappeared in rainbow hues, until the agitated water rested once more in a calm pool,
dimpled with sunlight, and overhung with
wild flowers.

But a terrible break and thundering fall at
last approached with rich Duncan Stewart,
from Lochaber! Duncan was a well-to-do
small tenant, with a number of beeves and
sheep; was a thrifty money-making bachelor
who never gave or accepted bills for man or
for best, but was contented with small pro-
fits, and ready cash secured at once and
hoarded in safety with Carrick, Brown, and
Company's Ship Bank, Glasgow, there to
grow at interest while he was sleeping—
though he was generally wide awake. He
was a cousin of Mary's, " thrice removed,"
but close enough to entitle him to command
a hearing in virtue of his relationship when
he came to court her; and on this very er-
rand he arrived one day at the manse, where
as a matter of course he was hospitably received—alas! for poor Donald Maclean.

Duncan had seen Mary but once, but having made up his mind, .which it was not difficult for him to do, as to her fair appearance, and having ascertained from others
that she was in every respect a most proper-

ly-conducted girl, and a most accomplished
servant, who could work in the field or dairy,
in the kitchen or laundry—that beside the
fire at night her hands were the most active in knitting, sewing, carding wool, or
spinning, he concluded that she was the very
wife for Duncan Stewart of Blairdhu. But
would Mary take him ? A doubt never
crossed his mind upon that point. His confidence did not arise from his own good
looks, for they, to speak charitably, were
doubtful, even to himself. He had high
cheek-bones, small teeth not innocent of to-
bacco, and a large mouth. To these features
there was added a sufficient number of grey
hairs sprinkled on the head and among the
bushy whiskers to testify to many more years
than those which numbered the age of Mary.
But Duncan had money, a large amount of
goods laid up for many years, full barns and
sheepfolds. He had a place assigned to him
at the Fort William market, such as a well-
known capitalist has in the City Exchange.
He was thus the sign of a power which tells

in every class of society.   Are no fair merchants' daughters, we would respectfully ask, affected in their choice of husbands by the state of their funds? Has a coronet no influence over the feelings? Do the men of substance make their advances to beauties without it, with no sense of the weight of argument which is measured by the weight of gold in their proffered hand? Do worth and character, and honest love and sufficient means, always get fair play from the fair, when opposed by rivals having less character and less love, but with more than sufficient means? According to the reader's replies to these questions will be his opinion as to the probability of Duncan winning Mary, and of Mary forsaking poor Donald and accepting his " highly respectable " and wealthy rival.

It must be mentioned that another power came into play at this juncture of affairs, and that was an elder sister of Mary's who lived in the neighborhood of the farmer, and who was supposed, by the observing dames of the

district, to have "set her cap" at Duncan.
But it was more the honor of the connection
than love which had prompted those gentle
demonstrations on the part of Peggy. She
wished to give him a hint, as it were, that he
need not want a respectable wife for the ask-
ing ; although of course she was quite happy
and contented to remain in her mother's
house, and help to manage the small croft,
with its cow, pigs, poultry, and potatoes.
Duncan, without ever pledging himself,
sometimes seemed to acknowledge that it
might be well to keep Peggy on his list as a
reserve corps, in case he might fail in his
first plan of battle. The fact must be confessed, that such marriages " of convenience " were as common in the Highlands as
elsewhere. Love, no doubt, in many cases,
carried the day there, as it will do in Green-
land, London, or Timbuctoo. Nevertheless,
the dog-team, the blubber, the fishing-tackle
of the North will, at times, tell very power-
fully on the side of their possessor, who is
yet wanting in the softer emotions ; and so

will the cowries and cattle of Africa, and the
West-end mansion and carriage of London.
The female heart will everywhere, in its own
way, acknowledge that "love is all very well,
when one is young, but—" and with that
prudential "but," depend upon it the blubber, cowries, and carriage are sure to carry
the day, and leave poor Love to make off
with clipped wings!

Duncan, of Blairdhu, so believed, when
he proposed to Mary, through the minister's
wife, who had never heard the kitchen gossip about the shepherd, and who was delighted to think that her Mary had the pros-
pect of being so comfortably married. All
the *pros* and *cons* having been set before
her, Mary smiled, hung her head, pulled her
fingers until every joint cracked, and, after
a number of "could not really says," and
"really did not knows," and "wondered
why he had asked her," and "what was she
to do," &c., followed by a few hearty tears,
she left her mistress, and left the impression
that she would in due time be Mrs. Duncan

Stewart. Her sister Peggy appeared on the scene, and, strange to say, urged the suit with extraordinary vehemence. She spoke not of love, but of honor, rank, position, comfort, influence, as all shining around on the Braes and Lochaber. Peggy never heard of the shepherd, but had she done so, the knowledge would have only moved her indignation. Duncan's cousinship made his courtship 'a sort of family claim—a social right. It was not possible that her sister would be so foolish, stupid, selfish, as not to marry a rich man like Mr. Stewart. Was she to bring disgrace on herself and people by refusing him? Mary was too gentle for Peggy, and she bent like a willow beneath the breeze of her appeals. She would have given worlds to have been able to say that she was engaged to Donald; but that was not the case. Would Donald ask her? She loved him too well for her to betray her feelings so as to prompt the delicate question, yet she wondered why he was not coming to.

her relief at such a crisis.   Did he know it ?
Did he suspect it ?

Donald, poor lad, was kept in ignorance
of all these diplomatic negotiations; and
when at last a fellow-servant expressed his
suspicions, he fell at once into despair, gave
up the game as lost, lingered among the
hills as long as possible, hardly spoke when
he returned home at night, seemed to keep
aloof from Mary, and one evening talked to
her so crossly in his utter misery, that next
morning, when Duncan Stewart arrived at
the manse, Peggy had so arranged matters
that Mary before the evening was understood to have accepted the hand of the rich
farmer.

The news was kept secret. Peggy would
not speak. Mary could not. Duncan was
discreetly silent, and took his departure to
arrange the marriage, for which the day was
fixed before he left. The minister's wife
and the minister congratulated Mary;
Mary gave no response, but pulled her fingers more energetically and nervously than

7

ever. This was all taken as a sign of modesty. The shepherd whistled louder than before for his dogs, and corrected them with singular vehemence; he played his trumps with greater perseverance, sang his best songs at night, but he did not walk with Mary from the kirk; and the other servants winked and laughed, and knew there was "something atween them," then guessed what it was, then knew all about it; yet none presumed to tease Donald or Mary. There was something which kept back all intrusion, but no one seemed to know what that something was.

The marriage dress was easily got up by the manse girls, and each of them added some bonnie gift to make Mary look still more bonnie. She was a special favorite, and the little governess with the work of her own hands contributed not a little to Mary's wardrobe.

All at once the girls came to the conclusion that Mary did not love Duncan. She had no interest in her dress; she submitted

to every attention as if it were a stern duty;
her smile was not joyous. Their suspicions
were confirmed when the cook, commonly
called Kate Kitchen, confided to them the
secret of Mary's love for the shepherd—all,
of course, in strict confidence; but every fair
and gentle attempt was made in vain to get
her to confess. She was either silent, or
said there was nothing between them, or she
would do what was right, and so on; or she
would dry her eyes with her apron, and
leave the room. These interviews were not
satisfactory, and so they were soon ended;
a gloom gathered over the wedding; there
was a want of enthusiasm about it; everyone
felt drifting slowly to it without any reason
strong enough for pulling in an opposite direction. Why won't Donald propose? His
proud heart is breaking, but he thinks it
too late, and will give no sign. Why does
not Mary refuse Duncan—scorn him, if you
will, and cling to the shepherd? Her little
proud heart is also breaking, for the shepherd has become cold to her. He ought to

have asked her, she thinks, before now, or
even now proposed a runaway marriage,
carried her off, and she would have flown
with him, like a dove, gently held in an
eagle's talon, over hill and dale, to a nest of
their own, where love alone would have de-
voured her.   But both said, " 'Tis too late !"
Fate, like a magic power, seemed to have
doomed that she must marry Duncan
Stewart.

The marriage was to come off at the house
of a Tacksman, an uncle of the bride's, about
two miles from the manse ; for the honor of
having a niece married to Blairdhu demanded special attention to be shown on the
occasion.   A large party was invited, a
score of the tenantry of the district, with the
minister's family, and a few of the gentry,
such as the sheriff and his wife ; the doctor ;
and some friends who accompanied Duncan
from Lochaber; big Sandy Cameron from
Lochiel ; Archy, son of Donald, from Glen
Nevis ; and Lachlan, the son of young Lachlan, from Corpach.   How they all managed

to dispose of themselves in the *but and ben*,
including the centre closet, of Malcolm Mor-
rison's house, has never yet been explained.
Those who have known the capacity of
Highland houses,—the capacity to be full,
and yet to be able to accommodate more, have
thought that the walls possessed some expan-
sive power, the secret of which has not come
down to posterity.. On that marriage day a
large party was assembled. On the green,
outside the house, were many Highland
carts, which had .conveyed their guests ;
while the horses, their fore-legs being tied
together at the fetlock, with ungainly hops
cropped the green herbage at freedom, until
their services were required within the next
twelve hours.   Droves of dogs were busy
making one another's acquaintance ; collie
dogs and terriers—every tail erect or curled,
and each, with bark and growl, asserting its
own independence. Groups of guests, in
homespun clothes, laughed and chattered
round the door, waiting for the hour of marriage. Some of " the ladies" were gravely

seated within, decked out in new caps and ribands; while servant-women, with loud voices and louder steps, were rushing to and fro, as if in desperation, arranging the dinner. This same dinner was a very ample one of stoved hens and potatoes, legs of mutton, roast ducks, corned beef, piles of cheese, tureens of curds and cream, and oat-cakes piled in layers. Duncan Stewart walked out and in, dressed in a full suit of blooming Stewart tartan, with frills to his shirt, which added greatly to his turkey-cock appearance.

But where was the bride? She had been expected at four o'clock, and it was now past five. It was understood that she was to have left the manse escorted by Hugh, son of big John M'Allister. The company became anxious. A message of inquiry was at last despatched, but the only information received was that the bride had left the manse at two o'clock, immediately after the manse party. A herd-boy was again despatched to obtain more accurate tidings, and the governess whispered in his ear to ask particu-

larly about the whereabouts of Donald the
shepherd. But the boy could tell nothing,
except that Hugh and the bride had started
on horseback three hours before; and as for
Donald, he was unwell in bed, for he had
seen him there rolled up in blankets, with
his face to the wall. The excitement became
intense. Duncan Stewart snuffed prodigi-
ously; Malcolm, Mary's uncle, uttered sundry expressions by no means becoming;
Peggy, full of alarming surmises, wrung her
hands, and threw herself on a bed in the
middle closet. The ladies became perplexed; the sheriff consulted the company
as to what should be done. The doctor
suggested the suicide of the bride. The
minister suspected more than he liked to express. But two men mounted the best horses, and taking a gun with them—why, no
one could conjecture—started off in great
haste to the manse. The timid bird had
flown, no one knew whither. The secret
had been kept from every human being.
But if she was to leave the parish it could

only be by a certain glen, across a certain
river, and along one path, which led to the
regions beyond. They conjected that she
was *en route* for her mother's home, in order
to find there a temporary asylum. To this
glen, and along this path, the riders hurried
with the gun. The marriage party in the
meantime "took a refreshment," and made
M'Pherson, the bagpiper, play reels and
strathspeys. Duncan pretended to laugh at
the odd joke—for a joke he said it was.
Peggy alone refused to be comforted. Hour
after hour passed, but no news of the bride.
The ladies began to yawn; the gentlemen to
think how they should spend the night; until at last all who could not be accommodated within the elastic walls by any
amount of squeezing, dispersed, after house
and barn were filled, to seek quarters at the
manse or among the neighboring farms.

The two troopers who rode in pursuit of
Mary came at last, after a hard ride of twenty
miles, to a small inn, which was the frontier
house of the parish, and whose white walls

McPherson, the Bagpiper.

Highlands.   p. 200.

marked, as on a peninsula, the ending of one long uninhabited glen, and the commencement of another. As they reached this solitary wayside place, they determined to put up for the night. The morning had been wet, and clouds full of rain had gathered after sunset on the hills. On entering the kitchen of the " change house," they saw some clothes drying on a chair opposite the fire, with a " braw cap " and ribands suspended near them, and dripping with moisture. On making inquiry they were informed that these belonged to a young woman who had arrived there shortly before, behind Hugh, son of big John M'Allister of the manse, who had returned with the horse by another road over the hill. The woman was on her way to Lochaber, but her name was not known. Poor Mary was caught! Her pursuers need not have verified their conjec tures by entering her room and upbraiding her in most unfeeling terms, telling her, before locking the door in order to secure her, that she must accompany them back in the

morning and be married to Duncan Stewart,
as sure as there was justice in the land.
Mary spoke not a word, but gazed on them
as, in a dream.

At early dawn she was mounted behind
one of these moss-troopers, and conducted in
safety to the manse, as she had requested to
see the family before she went through the
ceremony of marriage.   That return to the
manse was an epoch in its history.   The
shepherd had disappeared in the meantime,
and so had Hugh M'Allister.   When Mary
was ushered into the presence of the minister, and the door was closed, she fell on her
knees before him, and bending her forehead
until she rested it on his outstretched hand,
she burst forth into hysterical weeping.   The
minister soothed her, and bid her tell him
frankly what all this was about.   Did she
not like Stewart?   Was she unwilling to
marry him?   "Unwilling to marry him!"
cried Mary, rising up, with such flashing
eyes and dramatic manner, as the minister
had never seen before in her, or thought it

possible for one so retiring and shy to exhibit ; " I tell you, sir, I would sooner be chain-
ed to a rock at low water, and rest there until the tide came and choked my breath, than
marry that man !" and Mary, as if her whole
nature was suddenly changed, spoke out
with the vehemence of long-restrained freedom breaking loose at last in its own inherent
dignity. " Then, Mary dear," said the minister, patting her head, " you shall never be
married against your will, by me or any one
else, to mortal man." " Bless you, dear,
dear sir," said Mary, kissing his hand.

Duncan heard the news. " What on earth,
then," he asked; " is to be done with the dinner ?" for the cooking had been stopped. To
his Lochaber friends he whispered certain
sayings borrowed from sea and land—as, for
example : that there were " as good fish
in the sea as ever came out of it "—" that
she who winna when she may, may live to
rue't another day," and so on. He spoke and
acted like one who pitied as a friend the woman whom he thought once so wise as to

have been willing to marry Blairdhu. Yet Blairdhu's question was a serious one, and was still unanswered:—" What was to become of the dinner ?" Mary's uncle suggested the answer. He took Duncan aside, and talked confidentially and earnestly to him. His communications were received with a smile, a grunt, and a nod of the head, each outward sign of the inward current of feeling being frequently repeated in the same order. The interview was ended by a request from Duncan to see Peggy. Peggy gave him her hand, and squeezed his with a fervor made up of hysterics and hope. She wept, however, real tears, pouring forth her sympathies for the bridegroom in ejaculatory gasps, like jerks for breath, when mentioning a man of his " res — pect — a — bil — i — ty." Before night, a match was made up between Duncan and Peggy: she declaring that it was done to save the credit of her family, though it was not yesterday that she had learned to esteem Mr. Stewart; he declaring that he saw clearly the hand of Providence in the

whole transaction—that Mary was too young,
and too inexperienced for him, and that the
more he knew her, the less he liked her. The
hand of Providence was not less visible when
it conveyed a dowry of fifty pounds from
Peggy's uncle with his niece. The parties
were " proclaimed " in church on the following Sunday and married on Monday—and so
the credit of both the family and the dinner
was saved.

But what of Mary ?   She was married to
the shepherd, after explanations and " a
scene," which, as I am not writing fiction,
but truth, I cannot describe, the details not
having come to me in the traditions of the
parish.

Donald enlisted as a soldier in some Highland regiment, and his faithful Mary accompanied him to the Peninsula. How he managed to enlist at all as a married man, and
she to follow him as his wife, I know not.
But I presume that in those days, when soldiers were recruited by officers who had per-
sonally known them and their people, and to

whom the soldier was previously attached, many things were permitted and favors obtained which would be impossible now. Nor can I tell why Mary was obliged to return home. But the rules or necessities of the service during war demanded this step. So Mary once more appeared at the manse in the possession of about sixty pounds, which she had earned and saved by working for the regiment, and which Donald had intrusted, along with an only daughter, to his wife's care. The money was invested by the minister. Mary, as a matter of course, occupied her old place in the family, and found every other fellow servant, but Donald, where she had left them years before. No one received her with more joy than Hugh M'Allister, who had been her confidante and best man. But what stories and adventures Mary had to tell! And what a high position she occupied at the old kitchen fireside. Everything there was as happy as in the days of auld lang syne, and nothing wanting save Donald's blithe face and merry trumps.

Neither Mary nor Donald could write, nor could they speak any language except Gaelic. Their stock of English was barely sufficient to enable them to transact the most ordinary business. Was it this want, and the constant toil and uncertain marches of a soldier during war, which had prevented Donald from writing home to his wife? For, alas, two long years passed without her having once heard from him!

After months of anxious hope had gone by, Mary began to look old and careworn. The minister scanned the weekly newspaper with intense anxiety, especially after a battle had been fought, to catch her husband's name among the list of the dead or wounded. He had written several times for information, but with little effect. All he could hear was that Donald was alive and well. At last the news came that he was married to another woman. A soldier journeying homewards from the same regiment, and passing through the parish, had said so to several persons in the village, after he had had "his glass."

But the soldier was gone long before he could be cross-questioned. Mary heard the news, and though scorning the lie, as she said it was, the never alluded to the fearful story. Still the secret wound was evidently injuring her health; her cheek became paler, "the natural force abated" while at her work, and "Kate Kitchen" had on more than one occasion discovered tears dropping on the little girl's face as her mother combed her hair, or laid her down to sleep.

There was not a person in the house who did not carry poor Mary's burthen, and treat her with the utmost delicacy. Many an expression calculated to strengthen her faith in God, and to comfort her, was uttered at family prayers, which she always attended. Yet she never complained, never asked any sympathy; she was quiet, meek, and most unselfish, like one who tried to bear alone her own sorrow, without troubling others. She worked diligently, but never joined in the chorus song which often cheered the hours of labor. She clung much to Hugh M'Allister, who, like a shield, cast aside from her cruel darts which were shot in the parish by insinuations of Donald's unfaithfulness, or the repetition of the story "told by the soldier."

The fifth year of desolation had reached mid-summer, and it was clear that Mary was falling into permanent bad health. One day, having toiled until the afternoon at the making of a haystack, she sat down to rest upon some hay near it. Above, lads and lasses were busy trampling, under the super-intendence of Hugh M'Allister. Hugh sud-denly paused in the midst of the work, and gazing steadfastly for a minute or two at a distant person approaching the manse from the gate, said with a suppressed voice, and a "hush" which commanded silence, "If Donald Maclean is in life, that's him!" Every eye was directed to the traveller, who with knapsack on his back, was slowly ap-proaching. "It's a beggar," said Kate Kitchen.—"It's like Donald, after all," said another, as the sounds of the traveller's feet

were heard on the narrow gravel walk.—"It
is him, and none but him !" cried Hugh as
he slid down to the ground, having seen
Donald's face as he took off his cap and
waved it. Flying to Mary, who had been
half asleep from fatigue, he seized her by the
hand, raised her up, and putting his brawny
arm round her neck, kissed her ; then brush-
ing away a tear from his eye with the back
of his rough hand, he said, " God bless you !
this is better than a thousand pounds, any
day !" Mary, in perplexity and agitation,
asked what he meant, as he dragged her forward, giving her a gentle push as they both
came round the haystack which concealed
Donald from their view. With a scream
she flew to him, and as they embraced in silence, a loud cheer rose from the stack,
which was speedily hushed in silent sobs
even from the strong men.

What an evening that was at the manse !
If ever Donald heard the falsehood about his
second marriage, there was no allusion to it
that night. He had returned to his wife

and child with honorable wounds, a Water-
loo medal, and a pension for life. He and
Mary settled down again at the manse for
many months, and the trump was again
heard as in the days of yore.

I will not follow their adventures further,
beyond stating that they removed to Glasgow; that Donald died, and was buried
thirty years ago in the old church yard of
" the parish;" that the daughter was married, but not happily; that Mary fought a
noble, self-denying battle to support herself
by her industry, and her army savings, the
capital of which she has preserved until now.

When nearly eighty years of age she went
on a pilgrimage to visit Donald's grave.
" Do you repent marrying him," I asked her
on her return, " and refusing Duncan Stewart ?" " Repent !" she exclaimed, as her
fine old face was lighted up with sunshine;
" I would do it all again for the noble fellow ! "

Mary yet lives in Glasgow, respected by
all who know her.

XI.

The Grave of Flory Cameron.

WE might expect to find peculiar types of character among a people who possessed, as the Highland Celts do, a vivid fancy, strong passions, and keen affections; who dwell among scenery of vast extent and great sublimity; who are shut up in their secluded valleys, separated even from their own little world by mountains and moorlands or stormy arms of the sea; whose memories are full of the dark superstitions and wild traditions of the olden time; and who are easily impressed by the mysterious sights and sounds created by mists and clouds and eerie blasts, among the awful solitudes of nature; and who cling with passionate fondness to home and family, as to the very life and soul of the otherwise desert waste around them. But I never met, even in the Highlands, with a more remarkable example of the influence of race and circumstances than was Flora, or rather Flory Cameron.

The first time I saw her was when going to the school of "the parish," early on an autumnal morning. The school was attached to the church, and the churchyard was consequently near it. The churchyard, indeed, with its headstones and flat stones, its walled tombs and old ruined church, was fully appreciated by us, as an ideal place for our joyous games, especially for "hide and seek," and "I spy." Even now, in spite of all the sadder memories of later years, I can hardly think of the spot without calling up the blithe face of some boy peering cautiously over the effigy of an old chief, or catching the glimpse of a kilt disappearing behind a headstone, or hearing a concealed titter beside a memorial of sorrow.

As I passed the church yard for the first time in the sober dawning of that harvest day, I was arrested by seeing the figure of a woman wrapt in a Highland plaid, sitting on a grave, her head bent and her hands covering her face, while her body slowly rocked to and fro.   Beside her was a Highland terrier that seemed asleep on the grave. Her back was towards me, and I slipped away without disturbing her, yet much impressed by this exhibition of grief.

On telling the boys what I had seen, for the grave and its mourner were concealed at that moment from our view by the old ruin, they, speaking in whispers, and with an evident feeling of awe or of fear, informed me that it was " Flory the witch," and that she and her dog had been there every morning since her son had died months before ; and that the dog had been a favorite of her son's, and followed the witch wherever she went. I soon shared the superstitious fear for Flory which possessed the boys ; for, though they could not affirm, in answer to my inquiries, that she ever travelled through the air on a broomstick, or became a hare at her pleas-

ure, or had ever been seen dancing with de-
mons by moonlight in the old church, yet
one thing was certain, that the man or woman whom she blessed was blessed indeed, and
that those whom she cursed were cursed indeed. " Was that really true?" I eagerly
asked. " It is as true as death!" replied the
boy Archy Macdonald, shocked by my doubt
—" for," said he, " did not black Hugh Maclean strike her boy once at the fair, and did
she not curse him when he went off to the
herring fishery? and wasn't he and all in the
boat drowned? true! ay, it's true." " And
did she not curse," added little Peter M'Phie
with vehemence, " the ground officer for
turning old Widow M'Pherson out of her
house? Was he not found dead under the
rock? Some said he had been drunk; but
my aunt, who knew all about it, said it was
because of Flory's curse, nothing else, and
that the cruel rascal deserved it too." And
then followed many other terrible proofs of
her power, clinched with the assurance from
another boy that he had once heard " the

maister himself say, that he would any day
far rather have her blessing than her curse."

This conversation prepared me to obey
with fear and trembling a summons which I
soon afterwards unexpectedly received. Flory had one day, unseen by me, crossed the
playground, when we were too busy to notice
anything except the ball for which we were
eagerly contending at our game of shinty.
She heard that I was at the school, and seeing me, sent a boy to request my presence:
As I came near her, the other boys stood at a
respectful distance, watching the interview.
I put out my hand frankly, though tremb-
lingly, to greet her. She seized it, held it
fast, gazed at my face, and I at hers. What
she saw in mine I know not, but hers is still
vividly before me in every line and expression. It was in some respects very strange
and painfully impressive, yet full of affection.
—which appeared to struggle with an agon-
ized look of sorrow that ever and anon
brought tears down her withered cheeks.
Her eyes seemed at one time to retire into

her head, leaving a mere line between the
eyelashes, like what one sees in a cat when
in the light; they then would open slowly,
and gradually increase until two large black
orbs beamed on me, and I felt as if they drew
me into them by a mysterious power.
Pressing my hand with one of hers, she
stroked my head fondly, muttering to herself
all the time, as if in prayer.   She then said,
with deep feeling, "Oh, thou calf of my
heart! my love, my darling, son and grandson of friends, the blessed! let the blessing
of the poor, the blessing of the widow, the
blessing of the heart be on thee, and abide
with thee, my love, my love."   And then, to
my great relief, she passed on.   In a little
while she turned and looked at me, and, waving a farewell, went tottering on her way,
followed by the dog.   The boys congratulated me on my interview, and seemed to think
I was secure against any bodily harm. · I
think the two parties in our game that day
competed for my powerful aid. .

I often saw Flory afterwards, and instead

of avoiding her, felt satisfaction rather in having my hand kissed by her and in receiving the blessing, which in some kind form or other she often gave. Never, during the autumn and winter months when I attended that Highland school, did she omit visiting the grave on which I first saw her. The plashing rain fell around her, and the winds blew their bitter blast, but there she sat at early morning, for a time to weep and pray. And even when snow fell, the black form of the widow, bent in sorrow, was only more clearly revealed. Nor was she ever absent from her seat below the pulpit on Sunday. Her furrowed countenance with the strange and tearful eyes, the white *mutch* with the black ribbon bound tightly round the head, the slow rocking motion, with the old, thin, and withered body—all are before me though forty years have passed since then.

In after years, the present minister of the parish told me more about Flory than I then knew. The account given to me by the boys at school was to some extent true. She

was looked upon as a person possessing an
insight into the character of people and their
future, for her evil predictions had in many
cases been fulfilled. She had remarkable
powers of discernment, and often discovered
elements of disaster in the recklessness or
wickedness of those whom she denounced—
and when these disasters occurred in any
form, her words were remembered, and her
predictions attributed to some supernatural
communications with the evil one. Although
the violence of her passion was so terrible
when roused by any act of cruelty or injus-
tice, that she did not hesitate to pour it forth
on the objects of her hate, in solemn impre-
cations expressed in highly-wrought and po-
etic language, yet Flory herself was never
known to claim the possession of magic powers.* "She spoke," she said, "but the truth,

---

* In many Highland parishes—aye, and in Scotch and
English ones too—there were persons who secretly gave
charms to cure diseases and prevent injuries to man or
beast. These charms have come down from Popish

and cursed those only who deserved it, and
had they not all come true!"—Her violent
passion was her only demon possession.

---

times. A woman still lives in the "parish" who possessed a charm which the minister was resolved to obtain from her, along with the solemn promise that she
would never again use it. We understand that if any
charm is once repeated to and thus possessed by another,
it cannot, according to the law which regulates those
powers of darkness, be used again by its original owner.
It was with some difficulty that the minister at last pre-
vailed on "the witch" to repeat her charm. She did
so, in a wild glen in which they accidentally met. She
gave the charm with loud voice, outstretched arm, and
leaning against the stem of an old pine-tree, while the
minister quietly copied it into his note-book, as he sat
on horseback. "Here it is, minister," she said, "and to
you or your father's son alone would I give it, and once
you have it, it will pass my lips no more :—

"The charm of God the Great
   The free gift of Mary :
   The free gift of God :
   The free gift of every Priest and Churchman :
   The free gift of Michael the Strong?
   That would put strength in the sun."

Yet all this echo of old ecclesiastical thunder was but

Flory was not by any means an object of dislike. She was as ardent and vehement in her attachments as in her hates, and the former were far more numerous than the latter. Her sick and afflicted neighbors always found in her a sympathising and comforting friend. With that strange inconsistency by which so much light and darkness, good and evil, meet in the same character, Flory, to the minister's knowledge, had been the means of doing much good in more than one instance by her exhortations and her prayers, to those who had been leading wicked lives; while her own life as a wife and a mother had been strictly moral and exemplary. She had been early left a widow, but her children were trained up by her to be gentle, obedient, and industrious, and she gave them the best education in her power.

" a charm for sore eyes !" Whether it could have been used for greater, if not more useful purposes, I know not.

But it was God's will to subdue the wild
and impassioned nature of Flory by a series
of severe chastisements. When a widow, her
eldest son, in the full strength of manhood,
was drowned at sea; and her only daughter
and only companion died. One son alone,
the pride of her heart, and the stay of her
old age, remained, and to him she clung
with her whole heart and strength. He deserved, and returned her love. By his industry he had raised a sufficient sum of
money to purchase a boat, for the purpose
of fishing herring in some of the Highland
lochs—an investment of capital which in
good seasons is highly advantageous. All
the means possessed by Donald Cameron
were laid out on this boat, and both he and
his mother felt proud and happy as he launch-
ed it free of debt and was able to call it his
own. He told his mother that he expected to
make a little fortune by it, that he would
then build a house, and get a piece of land,
and that her old age would be passed under
his roof in peace and plenty. With many a

blessing from Flory his boat sailed away.
But Donald's partner in the fishing specula-
tion turned out a cowardly and inefficient
seaman. The boat was soon wrecked in a
storm. Donald, by great exertion, escaped
with his life. He returned to his mother a
beggar, and so severely injured that he sur-
vived the wreck of his boat and fortune but
a few weeks.

There was not a family in the parish
which did not share the sorrow of poor
Flory.

I have the account of his funeral now before me, written by one present, who was so
much struck by all he saw and heard on that
occasion that he noted down the circumstances at the time. I shall give them in his
own words :—

" When I arrived at the scene of woe, I
observed the customary preparations had
been judiciously executed, all under the immediate superintendence of poor Flory. On
entering the apartment to which I was con-

ducted, she received me with perfect com-
posure and with all that courteous decorum
of manner so common in her country. Her
dress she had studiously endeavored to ren-
der as suitable to the occasion as circumstances would permit. She wore a black woollen
gown of a peculiar, though not unbecoming
form, and a very broad black riband was
tightly fastened round her head, evidently
less with regard to ornament than to the ach-
ing pain implanted there by accumulated
suffering. In addressing the schoolmaster,
who had been assiduous in his parish atten-
tions towards her, she styled him the ' Coun-
sellor of the dying sufferer, the comforter of
the wounded mourner.' Another individual
she addressed as ' the son of her whose hand
was bountiful, and whose heart was kind,'
and in like manner, in addressing me, she
alluded very aptly and very feelingly to the
particular relation in which I then stood towards her. She then retired with a view of
attending to the necessary preparations
amongst the people assembled without the

house. · After a short interval, however, she returned, announcing that all was in readiness for completing the melancholy work for which we had convened. Here she seemed much agitated. Her lips, and even her whole frame seemed to quiver with emotion. At length, however, she recovered her former calmness, and stood motionless and pensive until the coffin was ready to be carried to the grave. She was then requested to take her station at the head of the coffin, and the black cord attached to it was extended to her. She seized it for a moment, and then all self-possession vanished. Casting it from her, she rushed impetuously forward, and clasping her extended arms around the coffin, gave vent to all her accumulated feelings in the accents of wildest despair. As the procession slowly moved onwards, she narrated in a sort of measured rhythm her own sufferings, eulogised the character of her son, and then, alas! uttered her wrath against the man to whose want of seamanship she attributed his death. I would it were in my

8

power to convey her sentiments as they were originally expressed.   But though it is impossible to convey them in their pathos and energy, I shall endeavor to give a part of her sad and bitter lamentation by a literal translation of her words.   Her first allusion was to her own sufferings.

"Alas!, alas! woe's me, what shall I do ?
  Without husband, without brother,
  Without substance, without store;
  A son in the deep, a daughter in her grave,
  The son of my love on his bier—
  Alas! alas! woe's me, what shall I do ?

  "Son of my love, plant of beauty,
  Thou art cut low in thy loveliness;
  Who'll now head the party at their games on the
      plains of Artornish ?
  The swiftest of foot is laid low.
  Had I thousands of gold on the sea-covered rock,
  I would leave it all and save the son of my love.
  But the son of my love is laid low—
  Alas! alas! woe's me, what shall I do ?

  "Land of curses is this !—where I lost my family and
      my friends,

My kindred and my store,
Thou art a land of curses for ever to me—
Alas! alas! woe's me, what shall I do?

" And, Duncan, thou grandson of Malcolm,
Thou wert a meteor of death to me;
Thine hand could not guide the helm as the hand of
    my love.
But, alas! the stem of beauty is cut down,
I am left alone in the world,
Friendless and childless, houseless and forlorn—
Alas! alas! woe's me, what shall I do?

" Whilst she chanted forth these and similar lamentations, the funeral procession arrived at the place of interment, which was
only about a mile removed from her cottage.
The grave was already dug.   It extended
across an old gothic arch of peculiar beauty
and simplicity.   Under this arch Flory sat
for some moments in pensive silence.   The
coffin was placed in the grave, and when it
had been adjusted with all due care, the attendants were about to proceed to cover it.
Here, however, they were interrupted. Flory
arose, and motioning to the obsequious
crowd to retire, she slowly descended into

the hollow grave, placed herself in an attitude of devotion, and continued for some time engaged in prayer to the Almighty.

" The crowd of attendants had retired to a little distance, but being in some degree privileged, or at least considering myself so, I remained leaning upon a neighboring grave-stone as near to her as I could without rudely intruding upon such great sorrow. I was, however, too far removed to hear distinctly the words which she uttered, especially as they were articulated in a low and murmuring tone of voice. The concluding part of her address was indeed more audibly given, and I heard her bear testimony with much solemnity to the fact that her departed son had never provoked her to wrath, and had ever obeyed her commands. She then paused for a few moments, seemingly anxious to tear herself away, but unable to do so. At length she mustered resolution, and after impressing three several kisses on the coffin, she was about to rise. But she found herself again interrupted. The clouds which had

been lowering were now dispelled, and just
as she was slowly ascending from the grave,
the sun burst forth in full splendor from behind the dark mist that had hitherto obscured
its rays. She again prostrated herself, this
time under the influence of a superstitious
belief still general in the Highlands, that
sunshine upon such occasions augurs well for
the future happiness of the departed. She
thanked God ' that the sky was clear and se-
rene when the child of her love was laid in
the dust.' She then at length arose, and resumed her former position under the old
archway, which soon re-echoed the ponder-
ous sound of the falling earth upon the hollow coffin.

"It was indeed a trying moment to her.
With despair painted on her countenance,
she shrieked aloud, in bitter anguish, and
wrung her withered hands with convulsive
violence. I tried to comfort her, but she
would not be comforted. In this full parox
ysm of her grief, however, one of the persons
in attendance approached her. 'Tears,'

said her friend, ' cannot bring back the dead. It is the will of Heaven—you must submit.' ' Alas !' replied Flory, ' the words of the lips —the words of the lips are easily given, but they heal not the broken heart !' The offered consolation, however, was effectual thus far, that it recalled the mourner to herself, and led her to subdue for the time every violent emotion. She again became alive to everything around, and gave the necessary directions to those who were engaged in covering up the grave. Her directions were given with unfaltering voice, and were obeyed by the humane neighbors with unhesitating submission. On one occasion indeed, and towards the close of the obsequies, she assumed a tone of high authority. It was found that the turf which had been prepared for covering the grave was insufficient for the purpose, and one of the attendants not quite so fastidious as his countrymen, who in such cases suffer not the smallest inequality to appear, proposed that the turf should be lengthened by adding to it. The observation did not escape her notice. Flory fixed her piercing eye upon him that uttered it, and after gazing at him for some moments with bitter scorn, she indignantly exclaimed, " Who talks of patching up the grave of my son ? Get you gone ! cut a green sod worthy of my 'beloved." This imperative order was instantly obeyed. A suitable turf was procured, and the grave was at length covered up to the entire satisfaction of all parties. She now arose, and returned to her desolate abode, supported by two aged females, almost equally infirm with herself, and followed by her dog.

" But Flory Cameron did not long remain inactive under suffering. With the aid of her good friend, the parish schoolmaster, she settled, with scrupulous fidelity, all her son's mercantile transactions ; and with a part of the very small reversion of money accruing to herself she purchased a neat freestone slab, which she has since erected as the ' Tribute of a widowed mother to the memory of a dutiful son.' Nor has her atten-

tion been limited to the grave of her son.
Her wakeful thoughts seem to have been the
subject of her midnight dreams. In one of
the visions of the night, as she herself
expressed it, her daughter appeared to her,
saying, that she had honored a son and
passed over a daughter. The hint was taken.
Her little debts were collected ; another slab
was provided on which to record the name
and merits of a beloved daughter; and to
his honor I mention it, that a poor mason
employed in the neighborhood entered so
warmly into the feeling by which Flory was
actuated that he gave his labor gratuitously
in erecting this monument of parental affection. But though the violence of her emotion subsided, Flory Cameron's grief long
remained. In church, where she was a regular attendant, every allusion to family
bereavement subdued her, and often, when
that simple melody arose in which her departed son was wont very audibly to join,
she used to sob bitterly, uttering with a low
tone of voice, 'Sweet was the voice of my

love in the house of God.' Frequently I
have met her returning from the burying-
ground at early dawn and at evening twi-
light, accompanied by her little dog, once
the constant attendant of her son ; and whilst
I stood conversing with her I have seen the
daisy which she had picked from the grave
of her beloved, carefully laid up in her
bosom. But her grief is now assuaged.
Affliction at length tamed the wildness of
her nature, and subdued her into a devo-
tional frame. She ceased to look for earthly
comfort, but found it in Christ. She often
acknowledged to me with devout submission
that the Lord, as He gave, had a right to
take away, and that she blessed His name ;
and that as every tie that bound her to earth
had been severed, her thoughts rose more
habitually to the home above, where God
her Father would at last free her from sin
and sorrow and unite her to her dear ones."

Flory continued to visit the grave of her
children as long as her feeble steps could
carry her thither. But her strength soon

failed, and she was confined to her poor hut.
One morning, the neighbors, attracted by
the howling of her dog, and seeing no
smoke from her chimney, entered unbidden,
and found Flory dead and lying as if in calm
sleep in her poor bed. Her body was laid
with her children, beneath the old arch.

XII.

The "Fools."

NO one attempting to describe from personal knowledge the characteristics of Highland life, can omit some mention, in memoriam, of the fools. It must indeed be admitted that the term "fool" is ambiguous, and embraces individuals in all trades, professions, and ranks of society. But those I have in my mind were not so injurious to society, nor so stupid and disagreeable, as the large class commonly called "fools." Nor is the true type of "fool," a witless idiot like the Cretin, nor a raving madman, fit only for Bedlam;—but "a pleasant fellow i' faith, with his brains somewhat in disorder."

I do not know whether "fools" are held in such high estimation in the Highlands as they used to be in that time which we call "our day." It may be that the Poor Laws have banished them to the calm and soothing retreat of the workhouse; or that the moral and intellectual education of the people by government pupils, and Queen's scholars, have rendered them incapable of being amused by any abnormal conditions of the intellect; but I am obliged to confess that I have always had a foolish weakness for "fools"—a decided sympathy with them— and that they occupy a very fresh and pleasing portion of my reminiscences of "the Parish."

The Highland "fool" was the special property of the district in which he lived. He was not considered a burthen upon the community, but a privilege to them. He wandered at his own sweet will wherever he pleased, "ower the muir amang and heather;" along highways, and bye-ways with no let or hindrance from parish beadles, rural police, or poor-law authorities.

Every one knew the "fool," and liked him as a sort of protégé of the public. Every house was open to him, though he had his favorite places of call. But he was too wise to call as a fashionable formal visitor, merely to leave his card and depart if his friend was "not at home." The temporary absence of landlord or landlady made little difference to him. He came to pay a visit, to enjoy the society of his friends, and to remain with them for days, perhaps for weeks, possibly for months even. He was sure to be welcomed, and never churled or sent away until he chose to depart. Nay, he was often coaxed to prolong the agreeable visit which was intended as a compliment to the family, and which the family professed to accept as such. It was, therefore, quite an event when some rare fool arrived, illustrious for his wit. His appearance was hailed by all in the establishment, from the shepherds, herds, workmen, and domestic servants, up to the heads of the family, with their happy boys and girls. The news spread rapidly from the kitchen to the drawing-room—" 'Calum,' 'Archy,' or 'Duncan' fool, is come!" and all would gather round him to draw forth his peculiarities.

It must be remembered that the Highland kitchen, which was the "fool's" stage, his reception and levee room, and which was cheered at night by his brilliant conversation, was like no similar culinary establishment, except, perhaps, that in the old Irish house. The prim model of civilised propriety, with its pure well-washed floors and whitewashed walls, its glittering pans, burnished covers, clean tidy fireside with roasting-jack, oven and hot plate, a sort of cooking drawing-room, an artistic studio for roasts and boils, was utterly unknown in the genuine Highland mansion of a former generation. The Highland kitchen had, no doubt, its cooking apparatus, its enormous pot that was hung from its iron chain amidst the reek in the great chimney; its pans embosomed in glowing peats, and whatever other instrumentality (possibly an additional peat fire on the floor) was required to prepare savory joints, with such barn-door dainties as ducks and hens, turkeys and geese—all supplied from the farm in such quantities as would terrify the modern cook and landlady if required to provide them daily from the market. The cooking of the Highland kitchen was also a continued process, like that on a passenger steamer on a long voyage. Different classes had to be served at different periods of the day, from early dawn till night. There were, therefore, huge pots of superb potatoes "laughing in their skins," and as huge pots of porridge poured into immense wooden dishes, with the occasional dinner luxury of Braxy—a species of mutton which need not be too minutely inquired into. These supplies were disposed of by the frequenters of the kitchen, dairymaids and all sorts of maids, with shepherds, farmservants male and female, and herds full of fun and grimace, and by a constant supply of strangers, with a beggar and probably a "fool" at the side-table. The kitchen was thus a sort of caravanserai, in which crowds of men and women, accompanied by sheep dogs and

terriers, came and went; and into whose pre-
cincts ducks, hens and turkeys strayed as often as they could pick up dèbris. The world
in the drawing-room was totally separated
from this world in the kitchen. The gentry
in " the room" were supposed to look down
upon it as on things belonging to another
sphere, governed by its own laws and customs, with which they had no wish to interfere. And thus it was that " waifs" and
" fools" came to the kitchen and fed there,
as a matter of course, having a bed in the
barn at night. All passers by got their " bite
and sup" in it readily and cheerfully. Servants' wages were nominal, and food was
abundant from moor and loch, sea and land.
To do justice to the establishment I ought to
mention that connected with the kitchen
there was generally a room called " the Servant's Hall," where the more distinguished
strangers—such as " the post" or packman,
with perhaps the tailor or shoemaker when
these were necessarily resident for some
weeks in the House—took their meals along

with the housekeeper and more "genteel" servants.

I have, perhaps given the impression that these illustrious visitants, the "fools," belonged to that Parish merely in which the houses that they frequented were situated. This was not the case. The fool was quite a cosmopolitan. He wandered like a wild bird over a large tract of country, though he had favorite nests and places of refuge. His selection of these was judiciously made according to the comparative merits of the treatment which he received from his many friends. I have known some cases in which the attachment became so great between the fool and the household that a hut was built and furnished for his permanent use. From this he could wander abroad when he wished a change of air or of society. Many families had their fool—their Wamba or jester—who made himself not only amusing but useful, by running messages and doing out-of-the-way jobs requiring little wit but often strength and time.

As far as my knowledge goes, or my memory serves me, the treatment of these Parish characters was most benevolent. Any teasing or annoyance which they received detracted slightly, if at all, from the sum of their happiness. It was but the friction which elicited their sparks and crackling fun; accordingly the boys round the fire-side at night could not resist applying it, nor their elders from enjoying it; while the peculiar claims of the fool to be considered lord or king, admiral or general, an eight-day clock or brittle glass, were cheerfully acquiesced in. Few men with all their wits about them could lead a more free or congenial life than the Highland fool with his wit only.

One of the most distinguished fools of my acquaintance was " Allan-nan-Con," or Allan of the Dogs. He had been drafted as a soldier, but owing to some breach of military etiquette on his part, when under inspection by Sir Ralph Abercromby, he was condemned as a fool, and immediately sent home. I must admit that Allan's subsequent career fully confirmed the correctness of Sir Ralph's judgment. His peculiarity was his love of dogs. He wore a long loose great-coat bound round his waist by a rope. The great-coat bagged over the rope, and within its loose and warm recesses a number of pups nestled while on his journey, so that his waist always seemed to be in motion. The parent dogs, four or five in number, followed on foot, and always in a certain order of march, and any straggler or undisciplined cur not keeping his own place received sharp admonition from Allan's long pike-staff. His head-dress was a large Highland bonnet, beneath which appeared a small sharp face, with bright eyes and thin-lipped mouth full of sarcasm and humor. Allan spent his nights often among the hills. "My house," he used to say, "is where the sun sets." He managed, on retiring to rest, to arrange his dogs round his body so as to receive the greatest benefit from their warmth. Their training was the great object of his life; and his pupils would have astonished any government inspector by their prompt obedience to their master's commands and their wonderful knowledge of the Gaelic language.

I remember on one occasion when Allan was about to leave "the Manse," he put his dogs, for my amusement, through some of their *drill*, as he called it. They were all sleeping round the kitchen fire, the pups freed from the girdle, and wandering at liberty, when Allan said, "Go out, one of my children, and let me know if the day is fair or wet." A dog instantly rose, while the others kept their places, and with erect tail went out. Returning, it placed itself by Allan's side, so that he might by passing his hand along its back discoverer whether it was wet or dry! "Go," he again said, "and tell that foolish child "—one of the pups—"who is frolicking outside of the house, to come in." Another dog rose, departed, and returned wagging his tail and looking up to Allan's face. "Oh he won't come, won't he? Then go and bring him in, and if necessary by force!" The dog again departed, but this time

carried the yelping pup in his mouth, and
laid it at Allan's feet. "Now, my dear
children, let us be going," said Allan, rising,
as if to proceed on his journoy. But at this
moment two terriers began to fight,—though
it seemed a mimic battle,—while an old sa-
gacious-looking collie never moved from his
comfortable place beside the fire. To understand this scene, though, you must know
that Allan had taken offence at the excellent
sheriff of the district because of his having
refused him some responsible situation on
his property, and to revenge himself had
trained his dogs to act the drama which was
now in progress. Addressing the apparently sleeping dog, whom he called " the
Sheriff," he said, " There you lie, you lazy
dog, enjoying yourself when the laws are
breaking by unseemly disputes and fights !
But what care you if you get your meat and
drink ! Shame upon you, Sheriff. It seems
that I even must teach you your duty. Get
up this moment, sir, or I shall bring my
staff down on your head, and make these

wicked dogs keep the peace!" In an in-
stant " the Sheriff" rose and separated the
combatants.

It was thus that, when any one offended
Allan past all possibility of forgiveness, he
immediately trained one of the dogs to illus-
trate his character, and taught it lessons, by
which in every house he could turn his supposed enemy into ridicule. A farmer, irritated by this kind of *dogmatic* intolerance,
ordered Allan to leave his farm. "Leave it,
forsooth!" replied Allan, with a sarcastic
sneer. "Could I possibly, sir, take it with
me, be assured I would do so rather than
leave it to you!"

When Allan was dying he called his dogs
beside him, and told them to keep him warm,
as the chill of death was coming over him.
He then bade them farewell, as his " children and best friends," and hoped they would
find a master who would take care of them
and teach them as he had done. The old
woman, in whose hut the poor fool lay, comforted him by telling him how, according to

the humane belief of her country, all whom
God had deprived of reason were sure to go
to heaven, and that he would soon be there.
"I don't know very well," said Allan, with
his last breath, "where I am going, as I
never travelled far; but if it is possible, I will
come back for my dogs; and, mind you," he
added, with emphasis, "to punish the Sheriff, for refusing me that situation!"

Another most entertaining fool was Donald Cameron. Donald was never more-bril-
liant than when narrating his submarine
voyages, and his adventures, as he walked
along the bottom of the sea passing from island to island. He had an endless variety
of stories about the wrecks which he visited
in the caverns of the deep, and above all of
his interviews with the fish, small and great,
whom he met during his strange voyages, or
journeys, rather. "On one occasion," I remember his telling me with great earnestness, as we sat together fishing from a rock,
"I was sadly put about, my boy, when coming from the island of Tyree. Ha! ha! ha,

It makes me laugh to think of it now, though
at the time it was very vexing. It was very
stormy weather, and the walking was difficult, and the road long. I at last became
hungry, and looked out for some hospitable
house where I could find rest and refreshment. I was fortunate enough to meet a
turbot, an old acquaintance, who invited me,
most kindly, to a marriage party which was
that day to be in his family. The marriage
was between a daughter of his own, and a
well-to-do flounder. So I went with the de-
cent fellow, and entered a fine house of
shells and tangle, most beautiful to see.
The dinner came, and it was all one could
wish. There was plenty, I assure you, to
eat and drink, for the turbot had a large fishing bank almost to himself to ply his trade
on, and he was too experienced to be cheated
by the hook of any fisherman, Highland or
Lowland. He had also been very industrious, as indeed were all his family. So he
had good means. But as we sat down to
our feast, and my mouth was watering—

just as I had the bountiful board under my
nose, who should come suddenly upon us
with a rush, but a tremendous cod, that was
angry because the turbot's daughter had accepted a poor thin, flat flounder, instead of
his own eldest son, a fine red-rock cod. The
savage, rude brute gave such a fillip with
his tail against the table, that it upset; and
what happened, my dear, but that the turbot, with all the guests, flounders, skate,
haddock, and whiting, thinking, I suppose,
that it was a sow of the ocean (a whale),
rushed away in a fright; and I can tell you,
calf of my heart, that when I myself saw the
cod's big head and mouth and staring eyes,
with his red gills going like a pair of fanners,
and when I got a touch of his tail, I was
glad to be off with the rest ; so I took to my
heels, and escaped among the long tangle.
I'fui! what a race of hide and seek that was!
Fortunately for me I was near the point of
Ardnamurchan, where I landed in safety,
and got to Donald M'Lachlan's house wet
and weary. Wasn't that an adventure?

And now," concluded my friend, " I'll put
on, with your leave, a very large bait of
cockles on my hook, and perhaps I may
catch some of that rascally cod's descendants ! "

" Barefooted Lachlan," another Parish
worthy, was famous as a swimmer. He
lived for hours in the water, and alarmed
more than one boat's crew, who perceived a
mysterious object—it might be the sea-ser-
pent—a mile or two from the shore, now appearing like a large seal, and again causing
the water to foam with gambols like those of
a much larger animal. They cautiously
drew near, and saw with wonder what
seemed to be the body of a human being
floating on the surface of the water. With
greatest caution an oar was slowly moved
towards it ; but just as the supposed dead
body was touched, the eyes, hitherto shut, in
order to keep up the intended deception,
would suddenly open, and with a loud shout
and laugh, Lachlan would attempt to seize

the oar, to the terror and astonishment of
those who were ignorant of his fancies.

The belief in his swimming powers—which
in truth were wonderful—became so exaggerated that his friends, even when out of
sight of land, would not have been surprised
to have been hailed and boarded by him. If
any unusual appearance was seen on the surface of the water along the coast of the Parish, and rowers paused to consider whether
it was a play of fish or a pursuing whale, it
was not unlikely that one of them would
at last say, as affording the most probable
solution, " I believe myself it is Barefooted
Lachlan !"

Poor Lachlan had become so accustomed
to this kind of fishy existence that he attached no more value to clothes than a merman
does. He looked upon them as a great practical grievance. To wear them on his aquatic
excursions was at once unnecessary and in-
convenient, and to be obliged, despite of
tides and winds, to return from a distant
swimming excursion to the spot on the shore

where they had been left, was to him an in-
tolerable bore. . A tattered shirt and kilt
were not worth all this trouble.   In adjusting his wardrobe to meet the demands of
the sea, it must be confessed that Lachlan
forgot the fair demands of the land.   Society at last rebelled against his judgment,
and the poor-law authorities having been
appealed to, were compelled to try the expensive but necesssary experiment of
boarding Lachlan in a pauper asylum in-
the Lowlands, rather than permit him to
wander about unadorned as a fish out of
water.   When he landed at the Breomie-
law, and saw all its brilliant gas lights,
and beheld for the first time in his life a
great street with houses which seemed pal-
aces, he whispered with a smile to his keepers, " Surely this is heaven ! am I right ?"
But when he passed onward to his asylum,
through the railway tunnel with its smoke
and noise, he trembled with horror, declaring that now, alas ! he was in the
lower regions and lost forever.   The .swim-

mer did not prosper when deprived of his long freedom among the winds and waves of Ocean, but died in a few days after entering the well-regulated home provided for his comfort by law. Had it not been for his primitive taste in clothes, and his want of appreciation of any better or more complete covering than his tanned skin afforded, I would have protested against confining him in a workhouse as a cruel and needless incarceration, and pleaded for him as Wordsworth did for his Cumberland beggar :

> As in the eye of Nature he has lived,
> So in the eye of Nature let him die !

While engaged in the unusual task of writing the biographies of fools, I cannot forget one who, though not belonging to " the Parish," was better known perhaps than any other in the Western Highlands. This man I speak of was " Gillespie Aotrom," or " light-headed Archy," of the Isle of Skye. Archy was perhaps the most famous character of his day in that island. When I made his acquaintance a quarter of a century ago, he was eighty years of age, and had been a notorious and much-admired fool during all that period—from the time, at least, in which he had first babbled folly at his mother's knee. Archy, though a public beggar, possessed excellent manners. He was welcomed in every house in Skye; and if the landlord had any appreciation of wit, or if he was afraid of being made the subject of some sarcastic song or witty epigram, he was sure to ask Archy into the dining-room after dinner, to enjoy his racy conversation. The fool never on such occasions betrayed the slightest sense of being patronised, but made his bow, sat down, and was ready to engage in any war of joke or repartee, and to sing some inimitable songs, which hit off with rare cleverness the infirmities and frailties of the leading people of the island—especially the clergy. Some of the clergy and gentry happened to be so sensitive to the power and influence of this fool's wit, which was sure to be repeated at " kirk and

market," that it was alleged they paid him
black-mail in meat and money to keep him
quiet, or obtain his favor. Archy's practical
jokes were as remarkable as his sayings.
One of these jokes I must narrate. An old
acquaintance of mine, a minister in Skye,
who possessed the kindest disposition and an
irreproachable moral character, was somewhat more afraid of Archy's sharp tongue
and witty rhymes than most of his brethren.
Archy seemed to have detected intuitively his
weak point, and though extremely fond of
the parson, yet often played upon his good-
nature with an odd mixture of fun and selfishness. On the occasion I refer to, Archy
in his travels, arrived on a cold night at the
manse when all its inmates were snug in bed,
and the parson himself was snoring loud beside his mate. A thundering knock at the
door awakened him, and thrusting his white
head, enveloped in a thick white nightcap,
out of the window, he at once recognized the
tall, well-known form of Archy. "Is this
you, Archy? Oich, oich! what do you

want, my good friend, at this hour of the night?" blandly asked the old minister. " What could a man want at such an hour, most reverend friend," replied the rogue, with a polite bow, "but his supper and his bed?" " You shall have both, good Archy," said the parson, though wishing Archy on the other side of the Coolins. Dressing himself in his home-made flannel unmentionables, and throwing a shepherd's plaid over his shoulders, he descended and admitted the fool. He then provided a sufficient supper for him in the form of a large supply of bread and cheese, with a jug of milk. During the repast Archy told his most recent gossip and merriest stories, concluding by a request for a bed. " You shall have the best in the parish, good Archy, take my word for it !" quoth the old dumpy and most amiable minister.

The bed alluded to was the hay-loft over the stable, which could be approached by a ladder only. The minister adjusted the ladder and begged Archy to ascend. Archy protested against the rudeness. " You call

that, do you, one of the best beds in Skye?
You, a minister, say so? On such a cold
night as this, too? You dare to say this to
me! " The old man, all alone, became
afraid of the gaunt fool as he lifted his huge
stick with energy. But had any one been
able to see clearly Archy's face, they would
have easily discovered a malicious twinkle
in his eye betrayed some plot which he had
been concocting probably all day. " I do
declare, Archy," said the parson, earnestly,
" that a softer, cleaner, snugger bed exists
not in Skye! " " I am delighted," said
Archy, " to hear it, minister, and must believe it since *you* say so. But do you know it
is the custom in our country for a landlord
to show his guest into his sleeping apartment, isn't it? and so I expect you to go up
before me to my room, and just see if all is
right and comfortable. Please ascend! "
Partly from fear and partly from a wish to
get back to his own bed as soon as possible,
and out of the cold of a sharp north wind,
the simple-hearted old man complied with

9

Archy's wish. With difficulty waddling up
the ladder, he entered the hay-loft. When
his white rotund body again appeared, as he
formally announced to his distinguished
guest how perfectly comfortable the resting-
place provided for him was, the ladder, alas!
had been removed, while Archy calmly remarked, "I am rejoiced to hear what you
say! I don't doubt a word of it. If it is so
comfortable a bedroom, though, you will have
no objection, I am sure, to spend the night
in it. Good night, then, my much-respected
friend, and may you have as good a sleep
and as pleasant dreams as you wished me to
enjoy." So saying, he made a profound bow
and departed with the ladder over his
shoulder. But after turning the corner and
listening with fits of suppressed laughter to
the minister's loud expostulations and earnest entreaties—for never had he preached a
more energetic sermon, or one more from his
heart—and when the joke afforded the full
enjoyment which was anticipated, Archy returned with the ladder, advising the parson

never to tell *fibs* about his fine bed-rooms again, but to give what he had without imposing upon strangers, he let him descend to the ground, while he himself ascended to the place of rest in the loft.

Archy's description of the whole scene was ever afterwards one of his best stories, to the. minister's great annoyance.

A friend of mine met Archy on the highway, and, wishing to draw him out, asked his opinion of several travellers as they passed. The first was a very tall man. Archy remarked that he had never seen any man before so near heaven! Of another he said that he had "the sportsman's eye and the soldier's step," which was singularly true in its description.

A Skye laird who was fond of trying a pass of arms with Archy, met him one day gnawing a bone. "Shame on you, Archy," "why do *you* gnaw a bone in that way?" "And to what use, sir," asked Archy in reply, "would you have me put it?" "I advise you," said the laird, "to throw it in

nevolent. At the same time I do not forget
another very different class, far lower in the
scale of humanity, which, owing to many circumstances that need not be detailed here,
was a very large one in the Highlands:—
creatures weak in body and idiotic in mind,
who in spite of the tenderest affection on
the part of their poor parents, were yet miserable objects for which no adequate relief
existed. Such cases indeed occur everywhere throughout the kingdom to a greater
extent than, I think, most people are aware
of. Those idiots are sometimes apparently
little removed above the beasts that perish,
yet they nevertheless possess a Divine nature never wholly extinguished, which is capable of being developed to a degree far beyond what the most sanguine could antici-
pate who have not seen what wise, patient,
benevolent and systematic education is capable of accomplishing. The coin with the
King's image on it, though lying in the dust
with the royal stamp almost obliterated, may
yet be found again and marvellously cleansed

and polished! I therefore hail asylums for idiot children as among the most blessed fruits of Christian civilisation. Though, strange to say, they are but commencing among us, yet I believe the day is near when they will be recognised as among the most needed, most successful, and most blessed institutions of our country.

XIII.

The Schoolmaster.

THE Parish Schoolmaster of the past belonged to a class of men and to an institution peculiar to Scotland. Between him and the Parish clergymen there was a close alliance formed by many links. The homes and incomes of both, though of very unequal value, were secured by Act of Parliament, and provided by the heritors of the Parish. Both held their appointments for life, and could be deprived of them only for heresy or imorality, and that by the same kind of formal "libel," and trial before the same ecclesiastical court. Both were members of the same church, and had to subscribe the same confession of faith; both might have attended the same university, nay, passed through the same curriculum of eight years of preparatory study.

The Schoolmaster was thus a sort of prebendiary or minor canon in the Parish cathedral—a teaching presbyter and coadjutor to his preaching brother. In many cases " the master" was possessed of very considerable scholarship and culture, and was invariably required to be able to prepare young men for Scotch universities, by instructing them in the elements of Greek, Latin, and Mathematics. He was by education more fitted than any of his own rank in the Parish to assoiciate with the minister. Besides, he was mostly always an elder of the kirk, and the clerk of the kirk session ; and, in addition to all these ties, the school was generally in close proximity to the church and manse. The master thus became the minister's right hand and confidential adviser, and the worthies often met. If the minister was a .bachelor—a melancholy spectacle too often seen !—the Schoolmaster more than any other neighbor cheered him in his loneliness.

He knew all the peculiarities of his diocesan,
and knew especially when he might "step
up to the Manse for a chat" without being
thought intrusive. If, for example, it was
Monday—the minister's Sunday of rest—
and if the day was wet, the roads muddy, the
trees dripping, and the hens miserable, seek-
ing shelter under carts in the farmyard, he
knew well that ere evening came, the minister would be glad to hear his rap break the
stillness of the manse. Then seated together in the small study before a cheerful
fire, they would discuss many delicate questions affecting the manners or morals of the
flock, and talk about ongoings of the Parish,
its births, marriages, and deaths; its poor,
sick, dying sufferers; the state of the crops,
and the prospects of good or bad "Fiars
prices," and the prospects of good or bad
stipends, which they regulated; the chances
of repairs or additions being obtained for
manse, church, or school; preachers and
preaching; Church and State politics—both
being out-and-out Tories; knotty theological

points connected with Calvinism or Armin-
ianism ; with all the minor and more evanes-
cent controversies of the hour. Or, if the
evening was fine, they would walk in the
garden to examine the flowers, or more probably the vegetables, and *dander* over the
glebe to inspect the latest improvements,
when the master was sure to hear bitter
complaints of the laziness of " the minister's
man" John, whom he had been threatening
to turn off for years, but who accepted the
threats with as great ease of mind as he did
his work.

A Schoolmaster who had received licence
to preach, and who consequently might be
presented to a parish, if he could get one,
belonged to the aristocracy of his profession.
Not that he lived in a better house than his
unlicensed and less educated brother, or received higher emoluments, or wore garments
less glittering and japanned from polished
old age.   But the man in the pulpit was
taller than the man in the school, addressed
larger pupils, and had larger prospects.

Among those Schoolmasters who were also preachers, it was possible, I dare say, to find a specimen of the Dominie Sampson class, with peculiarities and eccentricities which could easily account his failure as a preacher, and his equally remarkable want of success as a teacher. There was also a few, perhaps, who had soured tempers, and were often crabbed and cross in school and out of it. But don't be too severe on the poor Dominie! He had missed a church for want of a patron, and, it must be acknowledged, from want of the gift of preaching, which he bitterly termed "the gift of the gab." In college he had taken the first rank in his classes: and no wonder, then, if he is a little mortified in seeing an old acquaintance who had been a notorious dunce obtain a good living through some of those subtile and influential agencies, and "pow'r o' speech i' the poopit," neither of which he could command, and who—oleaginous on the tiends— slowly jogged along the smooth road of life on a punchy, sleek horse, troubled chiefly

about the great number of his children and
the small number of his " chalders ;" it is no
wonder, I say, that he is mortified at this,
compelled, poor fellow, to whip his way,
tawse in hand, through the mud of A B C
and Syntax, Shorter Catechism, and long
division, on a pittance of some sixty pounds
a year. Nay, as it often happened, the master had a sore ·at his heart which few knew
about. For when he was a tutor long ago
in the family of a small Laird, he fell in love
with the Laird's daughter Mary, whose mind
he had first wakened into thought, and first
led into the land of poetry. She was to have
married him, but not until he got a Parish,
for the Laird would not permit his fair star
to move in any orbit beneath that of the
Manse circle. And long and often had the
parish been expected, but just when the
presentation seemed to be within his nervous grasp, it had vanished through some unexpected mishap, and with its departure
hope became more deferred, and the heart
more sick, until Mary at last married,

and changed all things, to her old lover. She had not the pluck to stand by the master when the Laird of Blackmoss was pressing for her hand. And then the black curly hairs of the master turned to gray as the dream of his life vanished, and he awoke to the reality of a heart that can never love another, to a school with its A B C and Syntax. But somehow the dream comes back in its tenderness as he strokes the hair of some fair girl in the class and looks into her eyes; or it comes back in its bitterness, and a fire begins to burn at his heart, which very possibly passes off like a shock of electricity along his right arm, and down the black tawse, finally discharging itself with a flash and a roar into some lazy mass of agricultural flesh who happens to have a vulgar look like the Laird of Blackmoss, and an unprepared lesson!

It often happened that those who were uncommonly bad preachers, were, nevertheless, admirable teachers, especially if they had found suitable wives, and were softened

by the amenities of domestic life; above all
when they had boys of their own to "drill."
The Parish school then became a school of no
mean order. The glory of the old Scotch teacher of his stamp, was to *ground* his pupils
thoroughly in the elements of Greek and Latin.
He hated all shams, and placed little value
on what was acquired without labor. To
master details, to stamp grammar rules and
prosody rules, thoroughly understood, upon
the minds of his pupils as with a pen of iron;
to move slowly, but accurately through a
classic, this was his delight; not his work
only, but his recreation, the outlet for his
tastes and energies. He had no long-spun the-
ories about education, nor ever tried his
hand adjusting the fine mechanism of boy's
motives. "Do your duty and learn thoroughly, or be well licked," "Obedience,
work, and no humbug," were the axioms
which expressed his views. When he found
the boys honest at their work, he rejoiced in
his own. And if he discovered one who
seemed bitten with the love of Virgil or

Homer; if he discovered in his voice or look, by question or answer, that he "promised to be a good classic," the Dominic had a tendency to make that boy a pet. On the annual examination by the Presbytery, with what a pleased smile did he contemplate his favorite in the hands of some competent and sympathising examiner! And once a year on such a day the Dominie might so far forget his stern and iron rule as to chuck the boy under the chin, or clap him fondly on the back.

I like to call those old teaching preachers to remembrance. Take them all in all, they were a singular body of men; their humble homes, and poor salaries, and hard work, presenting a remarkable contrast to their manners, abilities, and literary culture. Scotland owes to them a debt of gratitude that never can be repaid; and many a successful minister, lawyer, and physician, is able to recall some of those old teachers as his earliest and best friend, who first kindled in him the love of learning, and hélped him in the pursuit of knowledge under difficulties.

In cities the Schoolmaster may be nobody, lost in the great crowd of professional and commercial life, unless that august personage the Government Inspector appears in the school, and links its master and pupil teachers to the august and mysterious Privy Council located in the official limbo of Downing Street. But in a country parish, most of all in a Highland Parish, to which we must now return, the Schoolmaster or "Master" occupied a most important position.

The Schoolmaster of "the Parish" half a century ago was a strong built man, with such a face, crowned by such a head, that taking face and head together, one felt that he was an out-and-out *man*. A Celt he evidently was, full of emotion, that could be roused to vehemence, but mild, modest, subdued, and firm,—a granite boulder covered with green moss, and hanging with flower, heather, and graceful fern. He had been three years at Glasgow University, attending the Greek, Latin, and logic classes. How he, the son of a very small farmer, had supported himself, is not easily explained. His fees, which probably amounted to 6*l*., were the heaviest item in his outlay. The lodgings occupied by him were in High Street, and he lived nearer the stars than men of greater ambition in Glasgow. His landlady, overlooking these peculiar privileges, charged but 4*s*. or 5*s*. a-week for everything, including coals, gas, cooking, and attendance. He had brought a supply of potatoes, salt herrings, sausages, and salt fish from the Highlands, and a ham which seemed immortal from the day it was boiled. It was wonderful how the student with a few pounds eked out his fare with the luxuries of weak coffee and wheaten bread for breakfast, and chop or mince-meat for dinner. And thus he managed, with a weekly sum which an unskilled laborer would consider wretched wages, to educate himself for three years at the University. He eventually became a schoolmaster, elder, session clerk, precentor, postmaster, and catechist of "the Parish," offices sufficient perhaps to stamp him as incompetent by the Privy Council Committee acting under "a Minute," but nevertheless capable of being all duty duly discharged by "the Master."

The school of course was his first duty, and there he diligently taught some fifty or sixty scholars in male and female petticoats for five days in the week, imparting knowledge of the "usual branches," and also instructing two or three pupils, including his own sons, in Greek, Latin, Mathematics. I am obliged to confess that neither the teacher nor the children had the slightest knowledge of physiology, chemistry, or even household economy. It is difficult to know, in these days of light, how they got on without it; for the houses were all constructed on principles opposed in every respect to the laws of health as we at present understand them, and the cooking was confined chiefly to potatoes and porridge. But whether it was the Highland air which they breathed, or the rain which daily washed them, or the absence of doctors, the children who ought to have died by rule did not, but were singularly robust and remarkably happy. In spite of bare feet and uncovered heads they seldom had colds, or, if they had, as Charles Lamb says, " they took them kindly."

His most important work next to the school was catechising. By this is meant, teaching the " Shorter Catechism " of the church to the adult parishioners. The custom was at certain seasons of the year, when the people were not busy at farm-work, to assemble them in different hamlets throughout the Parish : if the weather was wet, in a barn ; if fine, on the green hill side, and there by question and answer, with explanatory remarks, to indoctrine them into the great truths of religion. Many of the people in the more distant valleys, where even the small " side schools" could not penetrate, were unable to read, but they had ears to hear, and hearts to feel, and through these channels they were instructed. These meetings were generally on Saturdays when the school was closed. But on all days of the week the sick, who were near enough to be visited,—that is, within ten miles or so,— had the benefit of the master's teaching and prayers.

The Schoolmaster, I have said, was also postmaster. But then the mail was but weekly, and by no means a heavy one. It contained only a few letters for the sheriff or the minister, and half-a-dozen to be delivered as opportunity offered to outlying districts in the Parish, and these, with three or four newspapers a week old, did not occupy much of his time. The post, moreover, was never in a hurry. "Post haste" was unknown in those parts : the "Poste restante" being much more common. The "runner" was a sedate walker, and never lost sight of his feelings as a man in his ambition as a post. Nor was the master's situation as Precentor a position like that of organist in Westminster or St. Paul's. His music was select, and confined to three or four tunes. These he modulated to suit his voice and taste, which were peculiar and difficult to describe. But the people understood both, and followed him on Sundays as far as their own peculiar voices and tastes would permit; and thus his musical calling did not at all interfere with his week-day profession.

It is impossible to describe the many wants which he supplied and the blessings which he conferred. There were few marriages of any parochial importance at which he was not an honored guest. In times of sickness, sorrow, or death, he was sure to be present with his subdued manner, tender sympathy, and Christian counsel. If any one wanted advice on a matter which did not seem of sufficient gravity to consult about at the Manse, "the Master" was called in. If a trustee was wanted by a dying man, who would deal kindly and honestly with his widow and children, the master was sure to be nominated. He knew every one in the Parish, and all their belongings, as minutely as a man on the turf knows the horses and their pedigree. He was a true friend of the inmates of the Manse, and the minister trusted him as he did no other man. When the minister was dying the schoolmaster watched him by night, and tended him as an old disciple would have done one of the prophets, and left him not until with prayer he closed his eyes.

His emoluments for all this labor were not extravagant. Let us calculate. He had fifteen pounds as schoolmaster, five pounds in school fees, seven pounds as postmaster, one pound as session clerk, one pound as leader of church psalmody, five pounds as catechist—thirty-four pounds in all, with house and garden. He had indeed a small farm, or bit of ground, with two or three cows, a few sheep, and a few acres for potatoes and oats or barley, but for all this he paid rent. So the emoluments were not large. The house was a thatched cottage, with what the Scotch call a "butt and ben," the "butt" being half kitchen, half bedroom, with a peat fire on the floor, the "ben" having also a bed, but being dignified by a grate. Between them was a small bed closet separated from the passage by a wicker partition. All the floors were clay. Above was a garret or loft reached by a ladder, and containing amidst a dim light, a series of beds and shakes-down like a barrack. In this home father, mother, and a family of four sons and three daughters were accommodated. The girls learned at home—in addition to the " three r's " learned at school—to sew and spin, card wool, and sing songs; while the boys, after preparing their Virgil or arithmetic sums for next day, went in the evening to fish, to work in the garden or on the farm, to drive home the cattle, to cut peats for fuel or stack them, to reap ferns and house them for bedding the cattle in winter, or make composts for the fields, and procure moss and other unmentionable etceteras.

When darkness came they gathered round the fire, while some made baskets, repaired the horses' harness or their own shoes, or made fishing lines and " busked " hooks; others would discourse sweet music from the trump, and all in their turn tell stories to pass the time pleasantly. The grinding of meal for porridge or *fuarag* was a common occupation. This *fuarag* was a mixture made up of meal freshly ground from corn that had been well toasted and dried before the fire, and then whipped up with thick cream—a dainty dish to set before a king ! The difficulty in making it good was the getting of corn freshly toasted and meal freshly ground. It was prepared by means of a quern which at that time was in almost every house. The quern consisted of two round flat stones, of about a foot in diameter, and an inch or so thick, corresponding to the grinding stones in a mill. The lower stone was fixed, and the upper being fitted into it by a circular groove, was made to revolve rapidly upon it, while the corn was poured through a hole in the upper stone to be ground between the two. It was worked thus. A clean white sheet was spread over the bed in the kitchen. The mill was placed in the centre. One end of a stick was then inserted into a hole in the upper stone to turn it round, while the other end of the stick, to give it a purchase and keep it steady, was fixed in the twist of a rope stretched diagonally from one bedpost to another. The miller sat in the bed, with a leg on each side of the quern, and seizing the stack, rapidly turned the stone, while the parched corn was poured in. When ground it was taken away and cleared of all husks. The dry new meal being whipped up with rich cream the fuarag was ready, and then—lucky the boy who got it! I cannot forget the mill or its product, having had the privilege of often sharing in the labors of the one, and enjoying the luxury of the other.

Our Schoolmaster could not indeed give entertainments worthy of a great educational institute, nor did he live in the indulgence of any delicacies greater than the one I have dwelt upon, if indeed, there was any greater then in existence. There was for breakfast the never failing porridge and milk—and such milk !—with oat cakes

and barley scones for those who preferred
them, or liked them as a top-dressing.
On Sundays, there were tea and eggs.
The dinner never wanted noble potatoes with
their white powdery waistcoats, revealing
themselves under the brown jackets. At
that time they had not fallen into the
" sear and yellow leaf," but retained all
their pristine youth and loveliness as when
they rejoiced the heart of some Peruvian
Inca in the land of their nativity. With
such dainties, whether served up " each like
a star that dwelt apart," or mashed with
milk, or a little fresh butter, into a homogen-
eous mass, what signified their accompani-
ments?   Who will inquire anxiously about
them ?   There may have been sometimes
salt herring, sometimes other kinds of sea-fish
—lythe, rock-cod, mackerel, or saithe, but
oftener the unapproachable milk alone !   At
times a fat hen, and bit of pork, or blackfaced
mutton, would mar the simplicity of the dinner.   When these came, in Providence, they
were appreciated.   But whatever the food

all who partook of it ate it heartily, digested it with amazing rapidity, and never were the worse, but always the better for it. No one had headaches, or ever heard of medicine except in sermons; and all this is more than can bo said of most feasts, from those of the excellent Lord Mayor of London downwards, in all of which the potatoes and milk. are shamefully ignored, while salt herring and potatoes—the most savory of all dishes—and even fuarag, are utterly forgotten.

Handless people, who buy everything they require, can have no idea how the Schoolmaster managed to get clothes; yet they always were clothed, and comfortably, too. There was wool afforded by their own few sheep, or cheaply obtained from their neighbors, and the mother and daughter employed themselves during the long winter nights in carding and spinning it. Then Callum the weaver took it into hand to weave it into tartans, of any known Celtic pattern: and Peter the tailor undertook to shape it into comely garments for father or son; while the female tailors at home had no difficulty in arranging suitable garments out of their own portion of the wool. As for shoes, a hide or two of leather was purchased, and John the shoemaker, like Peter the tailor, would come to the house and live there, and tell his stories, and pour out the country news, and rejoice in the potatoes, and look balmy over the fuarag. Peter the tailor, when he went, left beautiful suits of clothes behind him; John the shoemaker completed the adornment by most substantial shoes—wanting polish probably, and graceful shapes, but nevertheless strong and victorious in every battle with mud and water, and possessing powerful thongs and shining tackets. And thus the family were clothed, if we except the kilts of the younger boys, which necessarily left Nature, with becoming confidence in her powers, to a large portion of the work about the limbs. The master's suit of black was also an exception. When that suit was purchased was a point not easily determined. It was generally understood to have been obtained when the Schoolmaster went on his first and last journey to see George IV. in Edinburgh. The suit was folded in his large green chest behind the door, and was only visible once a year at the communion, or when some great occasion, such as a marriage or a funeral, called it forth into sunlight. The tartan coat and home made woollen trousers were at such times exchanged for black broadcloth, and the black silk neckcloth for a white cravat; and then the Schoolmaster, with his grave countenance and grey whiskers, and bald head, might pass for a professor of theology or the bishop of a diocese.

The worthy Schoolmaster is long since dead. He died, as he had lived, in peace with God and man. The official residence has been changed to another part of the Parish, and when I last saw the once happy and contented home of the good man, with whom I had spent many happy days, the garden was obliterated, the footpaths covered with grass, and the desolation of many years was over it. Verily, the place that once knew him knew him no more.

XIV.

The Emigrant Ship.[*]

RETURNING from Iona on the loveliest summer evening which I ever beheld, we reached a safe and sheltered bay at the north end of the Island of Mull. I never saw a harbor so well defended from the violence of winds and waves. A long narrow island encircled it seawards, spreading its friendly wings over every vessel that comes to seek its covert from the storms of ocean, or to await under its shelter for favorable weather to double the great headland beyond. On the right hand where we entered, the land

---

* From the Gaelic of the late Rev. Dr. Macleod, of St. Columba's, Glasgow.

rises up steep and abrupt from the shore.
We sailed so close to the rocks, that the
branches of the trees were bending over us.
The fragrance of the birch was wafted on the
breeze of summer, and a thousand little birds
with their sweet notes, were singing to us
from amid the branches, bidding us welcome
as we glided smoothly and gently past them.
A glorious view presented itself to me wherever I turned my eye. I saw the lofty
mountains of Ardnamurchan clothed in
green to their very summits; Suanard, with
its beautifully outlined hills and knolls; the
coast of Morven stretching away from us, re-
joicing in the warmth of the summer evening.

When we neared the anchorage there was
nothing to be seen but masts of ships, with
their flags floating lazily in the gentle breeze
—nor to be heard, except the sound of oars,
and the murmur of brooks and streams, which,
falling over many a rock, were pouring into
the wide bay, now opening before us. From
side to side of the shore, on the one hand,

there runs a street of white houses ; and immediately behind them there rises up a steep bank, where the hazel, the rowan, and the ash grow luxuriantly, and so very close to the houses that the branches seem to bend over their tops. At the summit of this lofty bank the other portion of the small town is seen between you and the sky, presenting a view striking for its beauty and singularity.

The bay, however, presented the most interesting sight. There were in it scores of vessels of different sizes ; many a small boat with its painted green oars ; the gay *birlinn* with its snow-white sails, and the war-ship with its lofty masts and royal flag. But in the midst of them all I marked one ship which was to me of surpassing interest. Many little boats were pressing towards her, and I noticed that she was preparing to un-moor. There was one man in our boat who had joined us at the back of Mull, and who had not during the whole day, once head, but who now was scanning ship with the keenest anxiety.

10

"Do you know," I asked, "what this ship
is?"

"Alas!" said he, "'tis I who do know her.
Grieved am I to say that there are too many
of my acquaintances in her. In her are my
brothers, and many of my dearest friends, de-
parting on a long, mournful voyage for
North America. And sad is it that I have
not what would enable me to accompany
them."

We pulled towards the vessel; for I confess I felt strongly desirous of seeing these
warm-hearted men who, on this very day,
were to bid a last farewell to the Highlands,
in search of a country where they might find
a permanent home for themselves and families. It is impossible to convey to any one
who was not present, a true idea of the scene
which presented itself on going on board.
Never will it fade from my memory. They
were here, young and old—from the infant
to the patriarch. It was most overwhelming
to witness the deep grief, the trouble of
spirit, the anguish and brokenness of heart,

which deeply furrowed the countenances of the greater number of these men, here assembled from many an island and distant portion of the Hebrides.

I was, above all, struck with the appearance of one man, aged and blind, who was sitting apart, with three or four young boys clustered around him, each striving who could press most closely to his breast. His old arms were stretched over them; his head was bent towards them; his grey locks and their brown curly hair mingling, while his tears, in a heavy shower, were falling on them. Sitting at his feet was a respectably dressed woman, sobbing in the anguish of bitter grief; and I understood that a man who was walking backwards and forwards, with short steps and folded hands, was her husband. His eye was restless and unsettled, and his troubled countenance told that his mind was far from peace. I drew near to the old man, and in gentle language asked him if he, in the evening of his days, was about to leave his native land.

"Is it I, going over the ocean?" said he.
"No! On no journey will I go, until the
great journey which awaits us all; and when
that comes, who will bear my head to the
burial? You are gone; you are gone; to-day
I am left alone, blind and aged, without brother or son, or support. To-day is the day
of my desolation, God forgive me! thou
Mary, my only child, with my fair and lovely
grandchildren, art about to leave me! I will
return to-night to the old glen; but it is a
strange hand that will lead me. You, my
beloved children, will not come out to meet
the old man. I will no more hear the prattle
of your tongues by the river-side, and no
more shall I cry, as I used to do, though I
saw not the danger, 'Keep back from the
stream!' When I hear the barking of the
dogs, no more will my heart leap upwards,
saying, 'My children are coming.' Who
now will guide me to the shelter of the rock,
or read to me the holy book? And to-morrow night, when the sun sinks in the west,

where will you be, children of my love? or
who will raise the evening hymn with me?"

"Oh, father," said his daughter, creeping
close to him, "do not break my heart!"

"Art thou here, Mary?" said he. "Where
is thy hand? Come nearer to me. My delight of all women in the world. Sweet to
me is thy voice. Thou art parting with me.
I do not blame thee, neither do I complain.
Thou hast my full sanction. Thou hast the
blessing of thy God. As was thy mother before thee, be thou dutiful. As for me, I will
not long stand. To-day I am stripped of my
lovely branches, and light is the breeze
which will lay low my old head. But while
I live, God will uphold me! He was ever
with me in every trial, and He will not now
forsake me. Blind though I be, yet blessed
be His name! He enables me to see at His
own right hand my best Friend, and in His
countenance I see gentleness and love. At
this very moment He gives me strength. His
promises come home to my heart. Other
trees may wither; but the ' Tree of Life '

fades not. Are you all near me? Listen,"
said he, " we are now about to part. You
are going to a land far away ; and probably
before you reach it I shall be in the ·lofty
land where the sun ever shines, and where,
I trust, we shall all meet again ; and where
there shall be no partings, nor removals. No.
Remember the God of your fathers, and fall
not away from any one good habit which you
have learned. Evening and morning, bend
the knee. Evening and morning, raise the
hymn, as we were wont to do. And you, my
little children, who were as eyes and as a
staff unto me—you, who I thought would
place the sod· over me—must I part with
you? God be my helper ! "

I could not remain longer. The little boat
which was to bear the old man to the shore
had come to the side of the ship. Those who
were waiting on him informed him of this.
I fled ; I could not witness the miserable
separation.

In another part of the vessel there was a
company of men, whom I understood from

their dress and language to belong to the Northern Islands. They were keenly and anxiously watching a boat which was coming round a point, urged alike by sails and oars. Whenever they saw her making for the ship, they shouted out: "It is he himself! Blessings on his head!" There was one person among them who seemed more influential than the others. When he observed this boat, he went to the captain of the ship, and I observed that the sailors who were aloft among the masts and spars were ordered to descend, and that the preparations for immediate sailing were suspended. The boat approached. An aged, noble-looking man who was sitting in the stern, rose up, and, although his head was white as the snow, he ascended the side of the ship with a firm vigorous step, dispensing with any assistance. The captain saluted him with the utmost respect. He looked around him, and quickly noticing the beloved group who had been watching for him, he walked towards them. "God be with you!" he said to them, as they

all rose up, bonnet in hand, to do him reverence. He sat down among them. For a
while he leaned his head on the staff which
was in his hand, and I observed that great
tears were rolling down his face—one of the
most pleasant faces I had ever looked on.
They all grouped around him, and some of
the children sat at his feet. There was something in the appearance of this patriarchal
man which could not fail to draw one towards him. Such goodness and gentleness
surrounded him that the most timid would
be encouraged to approach him; and, at the
same time, such lofty command in his eye
and brow as would cause the boldest to quail
before him.

"You have come," said they, "according
to your promise; you never neglected us in
the day of our need. To-night we are to become wanderers over the face of the ocean,
and before the sun will rise over those hills
we shall be for ever out of their sight. We
are objects of pity to-day—day of our ruin!"

"Let me hear no such language," said the

minister. "Be manly; this is not the time for you to yield. Place your confidence in God: for it is not without His knowledge that you go on this journey. It is through His providence that all things are brought to pass; but you speak as if you were to travel beyond the bounds of the kingdom of the Almighty, and to go whither His Fatherly care could not extend unto you. Alas! is this all your faith?"

"This is all true," answered they; "but the sea—the great wide ocean?"

"The sea!" said he, "why should it cast down or disquiet you? Is not God present on the great ocean as on the land; under the guidance of His wisdom, and the protection of His power, are you not as safe on the wide ocean as you ever were in the most sheltered glen? Does not the God who made the ocean, go forth on its proud waves? Not one of them will rise against you without His knowledge. It is He who stills the raging of the sea. He goeth forth over the ocean in the chariots of the wind as surely as

He is in the heavens. Oh, ye of little faith, wherefore do ye doubt?"

"We are leaving our native land," said they.

"You are indeed leaving the place of your birth," he replied, "the island where you you were nourished and reared. You are certainly going on a long journey, and it need not be concealed that there are hardships awaiting you, but these do not come unexpectedly on you: you may be prepared to meet them. And as to leaving our country, the children of men have no permanent hold of any country under the sun. We are all strangers and pilgrims; and it is not in this world that God gives any of us that home from which there is no departure."

"That is undoubtedly true," said they; "but we go as 'sheep without a shepherd.' Without a guide to consult us in our perplexities. Oh, if you had been going with us!"

"Silence!" said he. "Let me not hear such language. Are you going further from

God than you were before? Is it not the
same Lord that opened your eyelids to-day
and raised you from the slumber of the night,
who rules on the other side of the world?
Who stood by Abraham when he left his
country and his kindred? Who showed himself to Jacob when he left his father's house,
and slept in the open field? Be ashamed of
yourselves for your want of trust. Did you
say you were as 'sheep without a shepherd'?
Is there any, even the youngest of your
children, who cannot repeat these words—
'The Lord 's my shepherd, I 'll not want'?
Has not the Great Shepherd of the sheep
said—'Fear not; for I am with thee. Be
not dismayed; for I am thy God'? Has
He not said—'When thou passest through
the waters I will be with thee; and through
the rivers, they shall not overflow thee'?
There are not, perhaps, houses of worship so
accessible to you where you are going, as
they were in your native land; nor are ministers of religion so numerous. But remember you the day of the Lord. Assemble

yourselves under the shelter of the rock, or under the shade of the tree. Raise up together the songs of Zion, remembering that the gracious presence of God is not confined to any one place; that, by those who sincerely seek Him in the name of Christ, He is to be found on the peak of the highest mountain, in the strath of the deepest glen, or in the innermost shade of the forest, as well as in the midst of the great city, or in the most costly temple ever reared by man's hands. You are all able to read the holy word. Had it been otherwise, heavy indeed would be my heart, and very sad the parting. I know you have some Bibles with you; but you will to-day accept from me, each a new Bible, one that is easily carried and handled; and you will not value them the less that your names are written in them by the hand which sprinkled the water of baptism on the most of you—which has often since been raised up to Heaven in prayers for you, and which will continue to be raised for you with good hope through Christ until death shall disable it.

And you, my little children, the precious lambs of my flock, now about to leave me, I have brought for you also some slight memorials of my great love to you. May God bless you !"

"Oh," said they, "how thankful are we that we have seen you once more, and that we have again heard your voice !"

The people of the ship were now generally gathered round this group, and even the sailors, though some of them did not understand his language, perceived it was in matters pertaining to the Soul he was engaged. There was so much earnestness, warmth, and kindliness in his appearance and voice, that they all stood reverently still; and I saw several of them hiding the tears which rolled down those cheeks that had been hardened by many a storm.

The reverend man uncovered his head, and stood up. Every one perceived his purpose. Some kneeled down, and those who stood cast their eyes downwards, when in a

clear, strong voice he said, " Let us pray for
the blessing of God." Hard indeed would
be the heart which would not melt, and little
to be envied the spirit which would not become solemnized, while the earnest, warm-
hearted prayer was being offered up by this
good man, who was himself raised above the
world. Many a poor faint-hearted one was
encouraged. His words fell like the dew of
the evening, and the weak, drooping
branches were strengthened and refreshed.

While they were on their knees I heard
heavy sighings and sobbings, which they
strove hard to smother. But when they rose
up I saw through the mist of the bitter tears
which they were now wiping off, the signs of
fresh hope beaming from their eyes. He
opened the Book of Psalms, and the most
mournful, the most affecting in every way,
yet at the same time the most joyful sacred
song which I ever heard was raised by them
all. The solemn sound reached every ship
and boat in the harbor. Every oar rested.

There was perfect silence; a holy calm as
they sang a part of the forty-second Psalm.

> " O ! why art thou cast down, my soul ?
>   Why, thus with grief opprest ?
>   Art thou disquieted in me ?
>   In God still hope and rest :
>   For yet I know I shall Him praise
>   Who graciously to me·
>   The health is of my countenance,
>   Yea, mine own God is He."

XV.

The Communion Sunday.

ON a beautiful Sunday in July I once
again sat down at the foot of the old
Iona-cross in the churchyard of "the Parish." It was a day of perfect summer glory.
Never did the familiar landscape appear
more lovely to the eye or more soothing and
sanctifying to the spirit. The Sound of Mull
lay like a sea of glass, without even a breath
of fitful air from the hills to ruffle its surface.
White sails met their own shadows on the
water; becalmed vessels mingled with grey
islets, rocky shores, and dark bays, diminish-
ing in bulk from the large brigs and schoon-
ers at my feet to the snow-white specks
which dotted the blue of the sea and hills of
Lorn. The precipice of Unnimore, streaked

with waterfalls, rose in the clear air above the old Keep of Ardtornish. The more distant castled promontory of Duart seemed to meet Lismore. Aros Castle, with its ample bay, closed the view in the opposite direction to the west; while over all the landscape a Sabbath stillness reigned, like an invisible mantle of love let down from the cloudless heaven over the weary world below.

It was a Communion Sunday in " the Parish."

Few of the people had as yet arrived, and the churchyard was as silent as its graves. But soon the roads and paths leading to the church from the distant glens and nearer hamlets began to stir with the assembling worshippers. A few boats were seen crossing the Sound, crowded with people coming to spend a day of holy peace. Shepherds in their plaids; old men and old women, with the young of the third generation accompanying them, arrived in groups. Some had left hours ago. Old John Cameron, with

fourscore-years-and-ten to carry, had walked
from Kinloch, ten miles across the pathless
hills. Other patriarchs, with staff in hand,
had come greater distances. Old women
were dressed in their clean white "mutches,"
with black ribands bound round their heads,
and some of the more gentle-born had rags
of old decency—a black silk scarf, fastened
with an old silver brooch, or a primitive
shaped bonnet—adornments never taken out
of the large wooden chest since they were
made, half a century ago, except on such occasions as the present, or on the occasion of
a family marriage feast, or a funeral, when a
bit of decayed crape was added. And old
men were there who had seen better days,
and had been gentlemen tacksmen in "the
good old times," when the Duke of Argyle
was laird. Now their clothes are threadbare;
the old blue coat with metal buttons is almost bleached; the oddly shaped hat and
silk handkerchief, both black once, are very
brown indeed; and the leather gloves,
though rarely on, are yet worn out, and can-

not stand further mending.   But these are gentlemen nevertheless in every thought and feeling.   And some respectable farmers from " the low country," who occupy the lands of these old tacksmen, travelled in their gigs. Besides these, there were one or two of the local gentry, and the assisting clergymen.

How quiet and reverent all the people look, as, with steps unheard on the green-sward, they collect in groups and greet each other with so much warmth and cordiality ! Many a hearty shake of the hand is given—and many a respectful bow, from old grey heads uncovered, is received and returned by their beloved Pastor, who moves about, conversing with them all.

No one can discover any other expression than that of the strictest decorum and sober thoughtfulness, among the hundreds who are here assembling for worship.

It has been the fashion indeed, of some people who know nothing about Scotland or her Church, to use Burns as an authority for calling such meetings " holy fairs."   What

they may have been in the days of the poet,
or how much he may himself have contributed to profane them, I know not. But neither
in Ayrshire nor anywhere else have I ever
been doomed to behold so irreverent and
wicked a spectacle as he portrays. The
question was indeed asked by a comparative
stranger, on the Communion Sunday I am
describing, whether the fact of so many people coming from such great distances might
not be a temptation to some to indulge over-
much when taking refreshments. The reply
by one who knew them well was, "No, sir,
not one man will go home in a state unbecoming a Christian."

The sentiment of gratitude was, naturally
enough, often repeated—"Oh! thank God
for such a fine day!" For weather is an ele-
ment which necessarily enters into every
calculation of times and seasons in the Highlands. If the day is stormy, the old and infirm cannot come up to this annual feast, nor
can brother clergymen voyage from distant
Island Parishes to attend it. Why, in the

time of the old minister, he had to send a
man on horseback over moors, and across
stormy arms of the sea, for sixty miles, to get
the wheaten bread used at the Communion !
And for this reason, while the Communion
is dispensed in smaller parishes and in towns
every six months, and sometimes every quarter, it has hitherto been only celebrated once
a year in most Highland Parishes. At such
seasons, however, every man and woman
who is able to appear, partakes of the holy
feast. No wonder, therefore, the people are
grateful for their lovely summer day !

The previous Thursday ad been, as usual,
set apart for a day of fasting and prayer.
Then the officiating clergyman preached specially upon the Communion, and on the character required in those who intended to
partake of it ; and then young persons, after
instruction and examination, were for the
first time formally admitted (as at confirma-
tion in the Episcopal Church) into full mem-
bership.

The old bell, which it is said was once at

Iona, began to ring over the silent fields, and
the small church was soon filled with worshippers. The service in the church to-day
was in English, and a "tent," as it is called,
(I remember when it was made of boat sails,)
was, according to custom, erected near the
old arch in the churchyard, where service
was conducted in Gaelic. Thus the people
were divided, and, while some entered the
church, many more gathered round the tent,
and seated themselves on the graves or on
the old ruin.

The Communion service of the Church of
Scotland is a very simple one, and may be
briefly described. It is celebrated in the
church, of course, after the service and prayers are ended. In most cases a long, narrow
table, like a bench, covered with white
cloth, occupies the whole length of the
church, and the communicants are seated on
each side of it. Sometimes, in addition to
this the ordinary seats are similarly covered.
The presiding minister, after reading an account of the institution from the Gospels and

Epistles, and giving a few words of suitable instruction, offers up what is called the consecration prayer, thus setting apart the bread and wine before him as symbols of the body and blood of Jesus. After this he takes the bread, and, breaking it, gives it to the communicants near him, saying, "This is my body, broken for you, eat ye all of it." He afterwards hands to them the cup, saying, "This cup is the New Testament in my blood, shed for the remission of the sins of many, drink ye all of it; for as oft as ye eat this bread and drink this cup, ye do show forth the Lord's death until He do come again." The bread and wine are then passed from the communicants to each other, assisted by the elders who are in attendance. In solemn silence the Lord is remembered, and by every true communicant is received as the living bread, the life of their souls, even as they receive into their bodies the bread and wine. During the silence of communion every head is bowed down, and many an eye and heart are filled, as the thoughts of Jesus at such a time mingle with those departed ones with whom they enjoy, in and through Him, the communion of saints. Then follows an exhortation by the minister to faith and love and renewed obedience; and then the 103d Psalm is generally sung, and while singing it the worshippers retire from the table, which is soon filled with other communicants; and this is repeated several times, until the whole service is ended with prayer and praise.

Let no one thoughtlessly condemn these simple services because they are different in form from those he has been accustomed to. Each nation and church has its own peculiar customs, originating generally in circumstances which once made them natural, reasonable, or perhaps necessary. Although these originating causes have passed away, yet the peculiar forms remain, and become familiar to the people, and venerable, almost holy, from linking the past with the present. Acquaintance with other branches of the Christian Church; a knowledge of living men,

and the spirit with which the truly good
serve God according to the custom of their
fathers; a dealing, too, with the realities of
human life and Christian experience, rather
than with the ideal of what might, could,
would, or should be, will tend to make us
charitable in our judgments of those who receive good and express their love to God
through outward forms very different from
our own. Let us thank God when men see
and are guided by true light, whatever may
be the form or setting of the lens by which
it is transmitted. Let us endeavor to penetrate beneath the variable, the temporary,
and accidental, to the unchangeable, the
eternal, and necessary; and then we shall
bless God when, among "different commu-
nions" and different sacraments, we can discover earnest believing souls, who have communion with the same living Saviour, who
receive with faith and love the same precious
sacrifice to be their life. I have myself, with
great thankfulness, been privileged to receive the sacrament from the hands of prie

and bishops in the rural churches and hoary cathedrals of England, and to join in different parts of the world, east and west, with brethren of different names, but all having the same faith in the One Name, of whom "the whole family in heaven and earth is named." I am sure the communion of spirit was the same in all.

Close behind the churchyard wall I noticed a stone which marked the grave of an old devoted Wesleyan minister. He was a lonely man, without any kindred dust to lie with. It had been his wish to be buried here, beside a child whom he had greatly admired and loved. "In memory," so runs the inscription, "of Robert Harrison, missionary of the Lord, who died 29th January, 1832. I have sinned; I have repented—I have believed, I love; and I rest in the hope that by the grace of God I shall rise and reign with my Redeemer throughout eternity." Beyond the churchyard are a few old trees surrounding a field where, according to tradition, once stood the palace of Bishop

Maclean. The Bishop himself lies under the old archway, near the grave of Flora Cameron. Now, I felt assured that could Wesleyan missionary and Episcopalian bishop have returned to earth, they would neither of them have refused to have remembered Jesus with these Presbyterian worshippers, nor would they have said "this is no true Sacrament."

When the service in the church was ended, I again sat down beside the old cross. The most of the congregation had assembled around the tent in the churchyard near me. The officiating minister was engaged in prayer, in the midst of the living and the dead. The sound of his voice hardly disturbed the profound and solemn silence. One heard with singular distinctness the bleating of the lambs on the hills, the hum of the passing bee, the lark "singing like an angel in the clouds," with the wild cries coming from the distant sea of birds that flocked over their prey. Suddenly the sound of

psalms rose from among the tombs.   It was
the thanksgiving and parting hymn of praise.

" Salvation and immortal praise .
　　To our victorious King.
　Let heaven and earth, and rocks and seas,
　　With glad hosannas ring !
　To Father, Son, and Holy Ghost,
　　The God whom we adore
　Be glory as it was and is,
　　And shall be evermore !"

So sang those humble peasants, ere they
parted to their distant homes—some to meet
again in communion here, some to meet at a
nobler feast above. So sang they that noble
hymn, among the graves of their kindred,
with whose voices theirs had often mingled
on the same spot, and with whose spirits
they still united in remembering and prais-
ing the living Saviour.

Some, perhaps, there are, who would have
despised or pitied that hymn of praise because sung with so little art. But a hymn
was once sung long ago, on an evening after
the first Lord's Supper, by a few lowly men
in an upper chamber of Jerusalem, and the

listening angels never heard such music ascending to the ears of God from this jarring and discordant world! The humble Lord who sang that hymn, and who led that chorus of fishermen, will not despise the praises of peasant saints; nor will the angels think the songs of the loving heart out of harmony with the noblest chords struck from their own golden harps, or the noblest' anthems sung in God's temple in the sky.

As the congregation dispersed, and the shades of evening began to fall, I went to visit the spot where the many members of the old Manse repose. A new grave was there, which had that week been opened. In it was laid the wife of the parish minister. This was the last of many a sad procession which he had followed from the old Manse to that burying-place since boyhood, and of all it was the most grievous to be borne. But of that sweet one so suddenly taken away, or of the bitter sorrow left behind, I dare not here speak.

These " reminiscences " began with death, and with death they end.

As I stood to-day among the graves of the Manse family, and sat in the little garden which its first-born cultivated as a child nearly eighty years ago, and as at midnight I now write these lines where so many beloved faces pass before me, which made other years a continual benediction, I cannot conclude my reminiscences of this dear old parish, which I leave at early dawn, without expressing my deep gratitude to Almighty God for his gift of those who once here lived, but who now live for evermore with Christ—enjoying an eternal Communion Sunday.

THE END.

Lightning Source UK Ltd.
Milton Keynes UK
UKHW020635050323
418046UK00007B/854